6/17

Brooks Free Library
739 Main St.
Harwich, MA 02645
(508) 430-7562

Antisocial

Antisocial

Jillian Blake

Delacorte Press

Text copyright © 2017 by Old Curiosity Shop, Inc.
Jacket photograph copyright © 2017 by Getty Images/David Ryle

Visit us on the Web! randomhouseteens.com

Educators and librarians, for a variety of teaching tools,
visit us at RHTeachersLibrarians.com

Library of Congress Cataloging-in-Publication Data is available upon request.
ISBN 978-1-101-93896-6 (trade) — ISBN 978-1-101-93897-3 (ebook) —
ISBN 978-1-5247-6470-8 (intl. ed.)

The text of this book is set in 12-point Berling.
Interior design by Ken Crossland

Printed in the United States of America
10 9 8 7 6 5 4 3 2 1
First Edition

Antisocial

1

IF I SEEM A LITTLE WIRED OR HIGH STRUNG OR JUST PLAIN OFF, don't worry. I'm not nuts. I just have a tendency to over-think every single thing that comes my way, ever. I suffer from what's known as social anxiety disorder, sometimes called social phobia. Big deal. So do fifteen million other people in America, or at least they will at some point in their lives, according to the Anxiety and Depression Association of America. I'll spare you the psychobabble. Basi-cally, a good number of my social interactions, both online and IRL, do bad, bad things to my nerves.

So you can probably guess how I'm feeling right now, in the dining hall at Alexandria Preparatory Academy, less than two weeks after my boyfriend dumped me and the whole world remembered that I'm socially irrelevant. That I'm not even close to being the cool, collected girl I've been passing for over the last three months.

My palms are so slippery that the tray I'm clutching like a religious offering may pop right out of my hands and fly across the room, trailing lunch behind it. I can hear the screams of laughter already. I close my eyes for a second and inhale through my nose.

Go somewhere calming in your mind, my therapist, Dr. Bechdel, would say in her soothing voice. I picture the volcanic black-and-snowy-white landscape of Vatnajökull Park in Iceland, feel the icy wind, not another soul in sight. Exhale, then open my eyes. One thing at a time. I've been working with Dr. Bechdel on it for months.

" 'Sup, Anna?" I hear at my three o'clock.

I turn just in time to see Dylan Johnson whiz by me. Then, as Dylan passes, another word comes out of his mouth. The word I spent all of Christmas break dreading, the word I've heard six times already today. That I can't stand hearing anymore.

"Sorry," he says without looking.

It's the first day back from winter break. The beginning of the end. Last semester of my high school career. It's an enviable position to be in, and you'd think that by now I'd have a million choices for where to sit in the Prep dining hall. But I don't have a million choices. I'm not sure I have any choices.

My *old* table—the one I sat at all of sophomore and junior years—is on the far left side of the dining hall. Nikki, Jethro, and Haven are yapping away, laughing and gesturing. Whatever they're talking about, I'd give my left ovary to be in on it. This is my mission now—*to get back there.*

Someday I'll convince them that I am not the biggest jerk in the history of Prep. I have to believe that.

Today I'll settle for sitting anywhere that people won't say *That Word* to me. And hopefully where people won't even look in my direction. The plan is simple: get to an empty table, take a few bites, get my blood sugar up, and show the world that *I'm still here.* That I'm down but not out.

I've run through this scene in my head—play by play, shot for shot, all possible outcomes—approximately 2.4 billion times since Christmas. But right now, bolting through the cafeteria is so tempting.

Stick to the plan, Anna. The plan is the only friend you have left.

I spot a table at the back. I can do this.

Mr. Fortini, the PE teacher, gives me a crinkly-eyed smile as he walks by. Great. Pitying looks from my teacher. At least he spared me an "It Gets Better" speech.

The first table I pass on my way to my *I am woman, hear me eat alone* home on the other side of the dining hall is the table of the drama crew, also known as the Thesbos. Most of them are run-of-the-mill hipsters, but some are dolled up for whatever YouTube vlog they're hosting after school.

After the Thesbos table is the Future Leaders of America table. They're the shiny-faced suck-ups in khakis and button-downs always trying to get you to vote for them for student council. Despite the fact that we're less than ten miles from D.C., school politics are dominated by people with an excess of optimism about the world. The good news today is that none of them seems to notice me.

"Sorry about your Christmas, Soler," some khaki wearer murmurs.

A stifled laugh follows.

Damn. Spoke too soon. My hands shake a little, but I clench the tray tighter and pretend I didn't hear anything.

The Hoodies have colonized the next table—a mix of techie, fanboy and fangirl comic-book types my (ex)-friends overlap with. The Hoodies smoke a lot of weed and are always telling you which concerts they've been to lately (featuring bands they may very well be making up, since no one has ever heard of them).

Just past the Hoodies, two boys are blocking my path to the eat-alone table.

"You're trying to tell me you've hit puberty, peewee?"

Wallace Reid, star center on the basketball team, is torturing a scrawny redhead. He's got him by almost a foot.

Only this kid isn't backing down as quickly as most of Wallace's victims. "I'm sorry," Scrawny says. "Having trouble understanding you. I'm only about fifteen percent fluent in meathead, according to my Rosetta Stone app."

Wallace laughs. "Man, you little white dudes crack me up."

Ms. Sozio, the pretty new dance teacher who graduated from Maryland just last spring, happens to be walking by and overhears. She wags a finger at Wallace and calls him to her as Scrawny scuttles to wherever he eats lunch. Wallace towers over Ms. Sozio as well, but now he leans down, and Ms. Sozio whispers in his ear. Whatever she says, Wallace's face now looks like a droopy dog's.

Ms. Sozio goes, and Wallace looks back toward his table.

The very table I have taken a blood-sworn oath to myself I wouldn't even look at. Only now Wallace catches my eye. "Anna," he says with a big smile. "How was your . . . break?"

Wonderful. He's mastered the art of wordplay.

"Look," he says, lowering his voice a register, "let's chill sometime, Anna. We'll talk about it, hang out. My parents are, like, never home."

"You . . . and me?"

"No reason not to anymore—am I right? Hey, Palmer's loss. But me, I've *always* dug South American girls. I dated a Brazilian hottie once. You knew that, right?"

Any normal person would ask if he was really trying to scam on his best friend's ex less than two weeks after Palmer and I broke up. But my tongue feels two times too big, and all I want is to make it to my empty table in back without anyone noticing. To die peacefully with my chicken salad sandwich.

I muster the best response I can. "Leave me alone, Wallace."

He claps his hands and gives me one of his famous *ooohs*, then grins and swaggers over to his table. The most valuable real estate in the dining hall.

Instagram Central.

Okay, I've denied you the most important group here at Prep long enough. The Instas are our version of the Beautiful People, who got their nickname by constantly posting pictures of themselves having crazy-fun times. They're the toned, cut-from-marble athletes of Prep's top-notch sports programs and their corresponding spirit squadders, plus a handful of, you know, absurdly good-looking and/or effortlessly cool nonathletes. Most people at school claim they loathe the Instas, but we're all kind of obsessed with them at the same time.

And for the past three months, I was sort of one of them.

Sort of.

What a difference a Christmas break makes. Palmer has lunch in a different period, but even so, I know all too well how weird it would be if I just strolled up to the Instas' table today. I wince, trying not to watch as Wallace says something inaudible to fellow jock Dylan Johnson and to Vanessa Eubanks, sandy-blond-haired captain of the spirit squad and unofficial queen of the Instas. She turns to look at me, and now a few other Instas do as well. Prickles go up and down my back. I always knew Vanessa thought I wasn't good enough for Palmer.

Now she's been proven right, I guess.

Prep is a small school. A lot of us have been going here since kindergarten. So Vanessa and I have known each other since we were six. And until about sixth grade or so, she was plain-looking and mostly kept to herself. It's not that she and I were *friends* then, exactly, but we acknowledged each other's existence. Which is a lot more than I can say about our relationship since then. Because when adolescence hit? *Boom.* Vanessa got hot. Tall. Gorgeous. And she learned the power of her family's wealth. Suddenly it was like everyone forgot that she was once a plain-Jane wallflower, and our whole grade has revolved around her ever since. She barely tolerated my guest appearances at the Insta table over the past months. She never asked me a single question about myself, and her minions—Alexis Bowman and Jocelyn van Mecl—weren't allowed to either.

Good thing they don't have to worry about tolerating my presence anymore.

"*Anna*. Hey."

I stop short and turn. Staring back at me is a pair of gray-green eyes.

"Oh," I say, caught in his gaze. "Hey."

Where do I start when it comes to Jethro Stephens? He's delicate featured and long lashed, with a mop of chin-length hair. He's grown into his skin-and-bones frame, so now he's tall with a nice, lanky body. So much has happened between Jethro and me, we could have a series on the History Channel.

He leans in and smiles a little. "On a scale of one to being forced to take part in a pep rally, how bad have your last three hours been?"

"Nine point nine."

"So it coulda been worse."

My pulse slows a little. My friendship with Jethro (before I bailed on it, anyway) has gotten . . . more and more complicated in the last couple of years. Twice we've gotten really close to kissing—sophomore year in his Jeep, junior year in my beat-up Honda (why does drama always go down in cars?)—but somehow it's never happened. Still, no matter how much things change between us, one thing's always been true: Jethro has a magical, *calming* effect on me. The same one he's having on me now.

"I meant to ask you," he says. "Did you see the Chuck Close exhibit?"

"What?"

"Chuck Close. He's one of your favorites, right? Did you make it to the exhibit?"

I shake my head, exhaling. "I wish. But the National Gallery over a holiday?"

I adore Chuck Close's portraits, but the massive crowds at D.C. museums and galleries are way too much for me. When I look at a painting, I tend to stare at it forever—to lose myself in it—and especially during tourist season I always feel like I'm loitering or in someone's way or doing something wrong. I end up spending the entire time worrying about what the museum-goers standing beside and behind me are thinking about me. How they're judging me. It is, in a word, miserable. Yeah, I know. If it sounds ridiculous, illogical, then you're starting to understand SAD.

Jethro smiles a little. "Yeah, I figured. Good." He reaches into his pocket and takes out a tiny black thing, then gently drops it on my tray. It's a thumb drive.

"Merry Christmas," he says. "Belated."

I smile. The first smile I've managed all day. I'm genuinely confused by Jethro being so nice to me right now, considering I basically ditched him the past three months.

"What's on it?" I ask.

"I took a video for you," Jethro says. "Got most of the pieces. They threw me out before I could get the Philip Glass portrait. But I got some good footage of Lou Reed."

There's always been something more than friendship

between us—something neither of us has acknowledged. Or probably ever will. But after I was a total and complete jerk for the past few months, I don't deserve this kindness. Or Jethro.

"Come sit with us," he says now.

I glance over at his table. "Probably not a good idea . . ."

"C'mon. It's a new year," Jethro says. He puts his arm around me, pressing his shoulder into mine. It makes me shiver. "Clean slate. For all of us."

He emphasizes one word slightly: *us*.

I've always (and when I say *always*, I mean most of the time, when my head's not up my you-know-what) taken pride in the fact that my group of friends doesn't have a label. It took me three months of hanging out with other, supposedly "cool" people to reinforce that they—this group of misfits—are the coolest people I know.

"Look what the holiday dragged in," Haven Dodd says as Jethro and I approach.

Nikki shifts in her chair, suddenly sitting a little more upright and formally than before. *"Anna,"* she says. Just that. Nothing else. I resist the urge to turn and run.

Nikki's blond, with a cute, smiley face and a dimple in her right cheek but not her left. Her figure is round and soft, and, though I think it's beautiful, she tries to hide it by crossing her arms over her chest or sucking in her stomach whenever a cute guy walks by. We've been friends since the first grade, and when I first started hanging out with Palmer, Nikki stuck with me. For the first month she'd still call me to watch *The Voice* or go shopping for the sweater Amandla Stenberg was wearing in that month's *Teen Vogue*. I'd either put her off with a lame excuse or say yes and then cancel at the last minute so I could see Palmer instead. Mostly, Nikki just seemed bewildered. She's such a good person that she couldn't conceive of one friend treating another so crappily.

Leave it to me.

I slide into the seat next to Jethro and set down my tray. Pretending to adjust the buckle on one of my boots, I hastily wipe my swampy hands on my leggings.

Think mountains in Iceland. Warm sunshine . . . black volcanoes . . .

"I heard the fam went skiing?" I ask Nikki, my voice even shakier than I expected it to be.

Nikki picks a carrot stick off her plate and dips it in hummus. "We had to come home early because my mom broke her arm."

"Wow. I didn't think Andrea actually skied."

"Yeah, that's not how she broke it. She made friends at the lodge with some of the other moms who don't ski. They had this long lunch with no food. None that they ate, anyway." Nikki rolls her eyes, then looks at the boys and makes a tippling gesture with her thumb and pinky finger. "She tripped getting off the elevator. She wears those fur boots with heels instead of, like, actual snow boots. Course, my stepdad wasn't there to help, so I wound up babysitting my brother, and then we all just went home."

This is going incredibly poorly. Nikki talking about

her mom's drinking—the one thing she never wants to discuss—means she's *really* uncomfortable.

"Yikes," I say. "Sorry, Nik."

"Yup," she says, apparently mesmerized by her hummus. "Me too."

"Don't worry, Anna," Haven says with a smile. "My break was even worse. I didn't get to violate *any* laws."

I play along. "Your dad was home the whole time?" Haven's dad is in the DEA. Intense in a way that is completely the opposite of Haven.

"Guy's a fascist. How am I supposed to do anything interesting when I'm only allowed on the computer an hour a day?"

Haven, whose claim to fame is being the school's best hacker, is a little weird-looking—skinny as a rail with a huge, bobbing Adam's apple, skin so pale it's almost translucent, and a dark kind of stringy hair that he really should get cut—but he has a cockiness that makes him homely-cute. And I'm sure he's smarter than most of the teachers at Prep, which also helps. He and Jethro are both going to MIT, planning to room together.

"But enough about us," Haven says with an impish smile. "I take it you win hands down for worst break, Anna. What happened with you and Bromeo?"

I finish chewing my bite of sandwich, glance at Jethro, and shrug. In the lightest voice I can muster, I say, "It's just over."

Haven looks like he might press me. But before he says anything else, a harsh voice interrupts us: "We're not talking to her."

11

I look up. Can an alien spaceship rip off the roof and beam me up *Guardians of the Galaxy*–style so I don't have to face what's next, please?

"Give her a break, Rad," Jethro says.

Rad is Radhika Mehta. She is—or I guess I should say *was*—my other best friend, also from first grade. Sandbox love never dies.

Unless, of course, you kill it, like I did.

Rad's dark-skinned like her father but has her mother's blue eyes and big breasts. Maybe she's not super hot by Insta standards, but she is by mine. Rad's also the most boy-crazy person I know. Or rather, I guess I should say *man* crazy, since Rad considers high school boys only useful for random hookups.

"Hey, Nik," says Rad. "Lemme ask you a question. How many times has Anna texted you in the last three months?"

When I start to open my open mouth, Rad flashes a palm at me like a stop sign.

Nikki stares at the tabletop, her cheeks filling with blood. "Not a whole lot," she says. She doesn't say it cruelly. Just matter-of-factly.

"I bet you can count the number of times on one hand and still have, like, a thumb and a couple fingers left over. And has she returned your calls? What's the average return time we're talking? A week? More?"

Like I said, Nikki was confused when I abandoned her. Rad, on the other hand, was *angry*. She stopped texting me and ignored me in the hallway. I heard from a couple of people that she wouldn't let anyone say my *name* around her.

Forcing myself not to cry and/or puke, I look Rad in the eye. "I'm sorry."

"Haven't you ever heard the expression *Hos before bros?*" Only Rad could pull off this question as seriously as I know she means it.

"C'mon guys," Jethro says. "Chill."

Haven chimes in. "You've all gotten caught up in dudes before."

Rad shakes her head. "Caught up? Or pathetically obsessed with a dude to the point of abandoning our best friends in our last year in high school together?"

Haven stares at Rad, blinks. "That was a mouthful."

Rad is the editor in chief of the school newspaper, the *Xandria*. So yes, she has a way with words. Everyone (but me) sort of chuckles, and Rad's face loosens up a little.

Grateful for the pause, I try to take advantage. "Look, I heard your announcement about the *Xandria* this morning," I start cautiously. "I was going to come to the meeting . . . if it's okay with you."

Rad shrugs. "Not like I can stop you. It's a free country." She waits a beat and then adds, "Unfortunately."

"What's unfortunate?" asks Andrew Yang, the last member of our group, as he slides in next to Jethro. A semi-jock, Andrew's the least misfitty of all of us: he's a lacrosse player; plus, his conservative Chinese parents don't let him grow his hair long or wear jeans with holes or anything like that.

Andrew lifts his thick eyebrows when he notices me. "Anna. You're here."

Before I can confirm, Rad asks, "Why *are* you here?

New Year's resolution to spend time with the little people? Give back to those less hashtag blessed?"

Is it conceivable she hasn't heard? Having to spit the words out to anyone, let alone to Rad, is more than I can handle today. My head is starting to pound, and everything sounds slightly underwater.

I manage a nod. "Palmer and I broke up."

Rad makes a snorting sound. "Yeah, *we know*, Benedict Arnold. We're not on another planet. I just figured you would find another Insta to latch on to."

"You're being kinda heartless," Andrew says.

She shoots him a look of death. "You ever want to see me naked again?"

Andrew shakes his head. "Come on."

"What do you think?" Rad surveys the table. "Am I being heartless? Because, see, I think Anna was the heartless one. Now that Palmer Meade is all done with her, I'm supposed to be jumping with joy that she's back? Give me a break."

I try to suck air in and find something, anything, to say back. "You're right. I'll just go. I'm sorry for messing up your lunch."

I get the words out, but the air isn't coming back in like it's supposed to. Something flutters in my chest. The beginning of a panic attack. Oh God, oh no, oh no, no, no. Not now. I take a breath, hold it in for three seconds, then let it out slowly as I stand up. New game plan: avoidance. I push my chair back.

"No, Anna," Jethro says. "Stay."

Now Haven raises his glass of chocolate milk to me as if

it's champagne. "I, for one, never look down on refurbished goods. Glad to have you back in the fold, babe." He has this weird way of being obnoxious and making you feel special all at once. Either way, I appreciate his easy forgiveness.

Rad glares at the guys. "I'm sorry, but I, for one, have had enough of her damsel-in-distress, wiggly-voice, panic routine." With that, she marches out of the dining hall.

Nikki glances at me, seems like she might say something. Like she might actually apologize for Rad's brashness, something she's been doing for as long as we've all known each other. Instead she picks up her tray and follows Rad out, making her loyalties clear. As I watch her go, I feel the prick of tears, the moisture pooling quickly in my eyes, so I open them wider and scrunch up my mouth to keep my chin from quivering Claire Danes–style. To make it worse, I can feel Jethro's eyes on me, and I know if I look back at him, the tears will be unstoppable.

But now I hear the soft sound of Jethro's voice in my ear. "Know what would be better than this place?" he asks.

He's the only other person who knows about my coping strategy, and he's giving me a lifeline. My mind races across the earth, searching, searching. Trying to find the perfect location. The other boys are talking among themselves, ignoring us for the moment. Or pretending to.

I look up at him. His face is so close to mine.

"Swimming with turtles in the Enchanted River," I say finally. "It's in the Philippines. They call it enchanted because the water looks like it was sprinkled with sapphire and jade. The indigenous people say it was done by fairies."

Jethro opens his lips, revealing the tiny, adorable gap

15

between his two upper front teeth. "I was thinking more like a hike and some camping between the stone towers in the Tianzi Mountain Reserve in China. The clouds hang over you like cotton puffs. You can paint the landscape while I make dinner over a fire."

He taps the table twice with the flat of his hand, then heads off with a smile.

2

You've probably figured me out by now: I'm *that* girl. The one who had friends she cared about, and who cared about her, for all of high school.

Who then screwed it all up when she fell for a boy.

Alexandria Prep—founded in 1904, motto Dare to Be True, known as Prep—has one of the best basketball teams in Virginia. The reason we're so good? The boy I fell for: Palmer Meade. The star power forward. The MVP. How did a girl with SAD who spends her time in the art lab end up dating the captain of the team, you ask?

Well, Palmer doesn't talk about it much, but we have a lot more in common than you might think. Palmer sleeps in his uniform the night before every single game. I once witnessed him worry himself sick (I stood outside the bathroom door) when he brought the wrong socks to wear for a game. Like, literally vomiting. He sweats through his sheets the nights before games and keeps track of every other promising recruit that Duke—his school of choice—is watching. He has a binder. It's intense.

Has he ever been diagnosed or treated? Nope. He's a star athlete. Guys like Palmer don't *have* "anxiety issues." They're just "superstitious." They have their rituals for success, and they might need a sports psychologist occasionally. But when you're getting recruited by the best colleges in the country, no one wants to know more.

So maybe Palmer liked that he and I could safely talk about his little "problem." Or maybe we just had that inexplicable chemistry. Whatever it was, for all of first semester, we were inseparable. I fell hard for a boy who seemed way out of my league.

Cliché, I know. But he was so sweet, so beautiful, so eager to learn about things he didn't know about—including my art and all the Colombian *fútbol* I watch with my dad. Soon I was consumed by him, swallowed way up. I wanted to be wherever he was. So I started watching basketball. Going to all his games. Having dinner with his parents and eventually spending more and more time with *his* friends. Which meant I was spending less and less time with my friends.

Including Jethro.

"How long till eighth period is over?" Andrew asks, puncturing a pudding-cup top with his spoon.

I snap back to attention. The cafeteria is emptying now. Everyone else at our table is gone. Andrew and I have been eating together, mostly in silence, for fifteen minutes.

"Well, there's about half an hour left in fifth," I say, grateful that he's talking to me. That *someone* is.

"I need weed if I'm making it to eighth," he says, sucking on a chocolaty spoon.

I could use some drugs myself. I went off daily antidepressants six months ago. SAD people aren't supposed to take them forever. Dr. Bechdel and I are focusing on therapy instead of my popping quick-fix Xanax, but right now I'd take anything.

"Rad'll get over it, by the way," Andrew says. "Someday."

"I wouldn't want you to lose hookup privileges on my account," I tell him.

"Please. Empty threats. You know that girl is horny as hell."

I do know that, and I'm about to respond when I notice there's an odd murmur around the dining hall. Prep has a strict cell phone policy, but half the kids in the room have their faces six inches from their illuminated screens, eyes wide and darting back and forth and up and down as they read things aloud to their friends. I see the chem teacher, Mrs. Bodkins, and the dance teacher, Ms. Sozio, and the few other teachers unfortunate enough to be on lunch duty flitting around in vain, trying to get people to put them away.

"What's up?" I wonder aloud.

Andrew's watching the weirdness in a daze, but he drops his spoon and whips out his Galaxy, which sits inside a plastic case with a picture of Zedd on it. How anyone can listen to EDM as much as he does is beyond me. We push our trays aside and lean over the table, heads close, to look at the screen.

According to the *To:* line, everyone at school has gotten the same email and attachment. Andrew opens the document, and at first I'm not sure what I'm seeing.

It's some kind of list . . . names and places and words and phrases and questions.

Jennifer Lawrence
itchy red bumps
easier quadratic equation
Jared Leto hair
Adele
nye party dc
keke palmer sexuality
suck stupid bitches
how hang besides netflix and chill
1D
5SOS
Forever 21 coupon codes
Batman vs. Superman
Demi Lovato
girl from *star wars*
birth control
homeroom origin definition
mixing medications
best hangover cure fast
how to get rid of puffy eyes
caffeine pregnancy

how to stop eating
life is so boring
husky puppies
best way to pop a zit
the Biebes
STD symptoms
fast easy hair
do colleges stop looking grades
second best ivy league
essay on Dostoyevsky free
give good head
game of thrones season 6 free
divorce mediation washington dc
redskins playoffs
calories in lettuce
knockoff kate spade
I hate school
how much weed is felony
first time anal

The list is more than thirty pages long, so there must be hundreds or maybe thousands of terms. Andrew swipes the list up and down like he's looking for something, or maybe he's just as confused as I am, having a hard time taking it all in.

"Whoa," Andrew says. "Weird."

I'm slow on the uptake, apparently, because I suddenly hear everyone else around me saying what Andrew quietly confirms: "It's searches. Like, Google searches."

"Whose?"

Andrew shrugs. "I mean. They look like things kids here'd search, don't they?"

Commotion is spreading across the dining hall. And laughter, so much laughter. A couple of people shout out search terms from one table to another, as if to say, *Was that you?*

I grab Andrew's phone.

Midway through the list, I see searches that look horrifyingly familiar.

how to fix a friend breakup
avoid rebounding with a close friend

I nod, swallow hard. There, smack in the middle of the list, are my very own, very private, very embarrassing searches from around nine-fifteen this morning, when I was hiding between classes in the Dwight Library bathroom, thinking about facing Rad and Nikki again, and—maybe most of all—preparing myself to see Jethro.

J and I spent so much of last summer together, when I needed him most. Without him I never would've gotten to the relatively healthy place that I'm in now (I know, I know, I still have *mucho* work to do). But then, just after Jethro helped me get back on my feet, Palmer happened. Palmer and I shared a bond through our anxiety, but he'd never seen me at my worst—I could let the past be past. With Jethro that's never been possible. He's seen too much.

My vision bends around the words like they're a fish-

22

eye camera lens, and my breath comes in little wheezing puffs that don't quite make it all the way to my lungs.

"What's up?" Andrew asks me.

"Nothing," I say. "These are just freaky. Someone recorded all these?"

"Someone," he says with a half smile.

Suddenly we hear a shriek from the Instas' table, and all eyes turn toward them. "Knockoff Kate Spade? *Knockoff?* I ask for *one thing* for my birthday, Joe, and you wanna get me a knockoff?" Maggie DeMarco, a junior on the spirit squad, is practically standing on her seat, shouting at Joe Tyler, a senior lacrosse player, who looks like he's shrinking with each shrill word. "Do you *know* how much that watch I got you for Christmas cost? Do you?"

"Who do you think did it?" I whisper to Andrew as we take in the scene.

"Haven." He gives me a shrug, like, *Who else?*

I stare back at the list as more commotion erupts around us.

Whoever it was, they're not making my long, painful climb back up the friendship ladder any easier.

3

WE'RE ALLOWED TO USE OUR PHONES AT SCHOOL ONLY WHEN there's an alert or update sent through the Prep scheduling-and-course app, so on a normal day, kids are usually ducking into bathroom stalls to see what snaps or texts or DMs or messenger alerts they've missed. But on my way to class, I pass seniors standing in front of their lockers, brazenly scrolling through the list on their phones and looking down the hall wild-eyed, starting rumors and trying to figure out who typed what. After four years, we seniors have learned to check and hide our devices like David Blaine working a deck of cards.

Around every corner I turn, I hear Haven being talked about:

". . . prolly can see what's on all our phones."

". . . hacked into the Department of Defense," one guy says.

"Someone needs to lock Haven Dodd in nerd jail," the junior whose locker is under mine is saying.

"That's not a thing . . . ," I murmur.

"'Scuse me?"

"Nothing." I slam my locker and hurry to class.

Did Haven actually do this one? He didn't seem particularly jumpy at lunch, but there's been plenty of hacking at school this year, and Haven and his fellow hacktivists are usually guilty somehow. Jethro's the only one who doesn't get involved—he's too worried about losing his place at MIT.

For the most part, what Haven does is funny. Most recently: right before Thanksgiving, during the Prep Spirit segment at assembly, he superimposed a photo of a turkey head on Vanessa Eubanks's face and distorted the audio so that she sounded like a kidnapper calling for ransom on one of those crime shows. Usually I can't stand assemblies, but I must've burned a hundred calories laughing at turkey-Vanessa.

A few randoms look in my direction as I head into the life-sciences wing. I focus harder on the floor in front of my feet. Someone must have matched me to my searches already. Oh God. I can't decide which one is more humiliating: *how to fix a friend breakup* or *avoid rebounding with a close friend*.

Ugh, couldn't I have waited until I got home?

Even if no one's pinned the searches on me yet, what'll happen after school, when everyone has a chance to really study the list? Then again, at least the Knock List—as it's already been named—seems to have pushed my breakup off the top ten most gossip-worthy things that have happened recently.

Environmental science passes in a blur—some smeary, colorful, sideways-moving activity: a student doing something with a soil sample and a petri dish, another student doing something with a pipette and a microscope, a teacher's voice *wah-wah-wah*ing in the background, markers squeaking across the whiteboard.

And by eighth period I still haven't run into Palmer.

Here's to small mercies.

The one thing that will truly make me breathe easy is being in the art lab. I need to work on my senior project, anyway—and painting helps me unwind, even more than Xanax. As I hightail it through the senior lounge, avoiding eye contact with my peers, I can't help but notice Nikki standing in a small circle with Mattie Eizenberg and some of his Insta-crossover friends.

"I hate this place. . . . Prep is dead to me," Mattie's mimicking with his slight Southern lilt. "Think how pathetic it is . . . people just typing in random shit they feel. It's like Google is their therapist!"

Some of the girls around him laugh, even though it's not that funny. Mattie's striking white-blond hair, which he always keeps up in a perfect man bun, combined with his flair for the stage make him a natural for the lead role of Puck in *A Midsummer Night's Dream*, the spring play. He spends a lot of time in tights for the role, but he's not gay. Au contraire. He's a Thesbo, yes, but he's good-looking enough that even some of the Insta girls sometimes vie for his attention.

"I read about how people type hate stuff into Google," Nikki interjects. "Like, they actually type *I hate Muslims* after terrorist attacks. Can you believe it? I mean, what are they looking for? Other idiots who hate Muslims? It's the dumbest thing ever."

Mattie looks at her, flashes that someday-Oscar-winning smile. "Land of the free, home of the stupid."

Nikki looks at the floor, beaming, flattered that Mattie's validating her.

She's been "in love" with Mattie for all of high school, and she's been committed to losing her virginity to him since junior year. I've never been Mattie's biggest fan, and as far as I can tell, he's never wanted to hang out with Nikki before. But the way he's looking at her now—maybe there's hope for her. She joined the stage crew for the play just to get closer to him. Maybe it's working.

I just hope she's careful. Nik's not one of those done-everything-but-It virgins. She's been kissed a bunch of times, and she's been to second base once. Something about Mattie gives me the feeling that she wouldn't be *his* first.

Nikki looks up, and we make eye contact, but the smile melts right off her face. She turns back to Mattie without even a second glance. *O-kay,* guess that whole abandoning-me-in-the-cafeteria thing this afternoon wasn't just a one-time event.

Buzzzzzz.

The room freezes, and everyone looks up at the loud-speaker installed in the corner of the lounge. *"Attention, students."* Headmaster Nichols's dull voice hangs in the air.

"Due to a small glitch on the Prep for Today application, certain search data was accidentally . . . cached this morning, and some students in the computer science lab acted inappropriately by passing this information to the Prep contact list. Please delete the email immediately when you get home. I'd like to remind you that cell phones, tablets, and other unauthorized devices are not allowed to be used during the school day, and we will hold detention in the chapel, should we need the space. Thank you."

When the announcement ends, the senior lounge returns to its usual hellish cacophony. People are laughing, mocking Nichols, comparing notes about this revelation, debating whether Nichols is telling the truth and this really was some kind of glitch, or whether the school IT guys don't want to admit they got hacked.

"Not a mouse / Shall disturb this hallow'd house: / I am sent with broom before, / To sweep the dust behind the door," Mattie performs for the room.

My favorite teacher, Mr. Touhey, has curly gray-brown hair and a mustache. He calls his favorites *kiddo* and keeps class pretty loose. All of us in Advanced Art actually want to be here, so he mostly just lets us spend the period working on our projects while he hangs out at the back of the room in a flannel button-down, Doc Marten boots crossed at the ankles and propped up on his desk, reading old issues of *Artforum* and *Juxtapoz* and eating from an enormous ziplock bag of trail mix, available if we have any problems or questions or just want to, as he refers to it, rap.

"Hiya, kiddo," Mr. Touhey says as I enter the room. "How was your break?"

"Broke up with my boyfriend. So, you know, fabulous."

He blinks a couple of times in rapid succession. "Hmmm. That Meeks kid?"

"Meade."

"Well. Pain is the path to the sublime. Just ask . . . Van Gogh. You should just put the *pain* into your *pain*ting."

I smile and roll my eyes at his pun. "I'm not really *in* pain, to be honest. I'm just kind of . . . numb."

Touhey shrugs. "Oh well, you'll have to find inspiration elsewhere, I guess."

"My friends hate me. So there's that," I say.

A flash of actual concern spreads across Mr. Touhey's face. Per Dr. Bechdel's order, all my teachers know about my anxiety, though most of them treat me no differently from any other socially well-adjusted student. Thank God.

"Well," he says, "channel *that* today, then. And I'm here if you need to talk."

Heading to the wall hooks to hang up my backpack, I pass Kyle Cherski, already bent over a worktable and his trusty iPad. I guess I'd call Kyle a goth-dork hybrid, and that's if I'm being nice. Right now he's laboring over one of his patented digital drawings that he does using nothing but his eyes and an iPad stylus. The images on his screen look like things you'd see in a comic book, the porno-violent kind that disaffected teenage boys read: women with whips, guys with big muscles and bigger guns, gangs of roaming hooligans and greasers facing off on the rain-slicked streets of some nightmare cityscape. It isn't for me, and hell on earth would be drawing only on a screen, but his skill is undeniable.

"Wow," I say. "That's crazy good, Kyle."

He doesn't lift his head, but he nods. "Yeah."

"Imagine what you could do with actual ink."

"But that wouldn't be fair to everyone else."

I snort and grab my three-by-five canvas from the storage cubby. I wish I had Kyle's confidence. I mean, I *did* apply early to art school. Rhode Island School of Design is my top choice. But I haven't heard back yet. Now my senior project, the one I've been working on all year and the one I'm supposed to be showing at the art show in two weeks, feels somehow . . . flawed.

Maybe it's my *subject* that's the problem.

It's an oil self-portrait tentatively titled *Antisocial*. In it, I'm doing my best Kardashian pout, staring up and directly into the viewer's perspective. The slightly elevated, close-up angle is a familiar one—same as with a selfie stick. When we play the *Which celebrity do you most resemble?* game, my friends say I look like a young Sofía Vergara, but I think that's just because she's the only Colombian outside of Shakira or Pablo Escobar any of them have heard of. I don't actually look anything like her.

When I started this project, it all made sense to me. I wanted to say something about our narcissism, about how the value of the self-image has changed so much with our generation. But as I stare at the canvas today, I know there's something not quite right about it. It's as if, after a couple of weeks away, my selfie portrait suddenly feels painfully, horribly *obvious*. Like, *yes*, we're all narcissists—what about it?

I'm unscrewing the tube of azure Sennelier, hoping inspiration will strike, when I catch a glimpse of movement inside the doorway in my peripheral vision.

Jethro took art last year and knows Mr. Touhey well, so he passes inside with a polite wave, and now he's walking toward me. I can't help but notice that the other girls in the lab look up. Jethro's officially a babe. That postpubescent gawkiness? Gone. He moves comfortably, coolly, in his body. The longer hair suits him too.

I move toward him, quickly cutting him off from my station. No way am I letting him see my selfie portrait; I'm not in the mood to accept whatever compliment Jethro will inevitably give me, especially when I know the piece is crap and I don't deserve it.

"Hey. Can we talk?" he asks gently.

"Of course. Everything okay?"

He ushers me into the empty hallway. As we stand face to face by the slate-gray wall, I tip my head back slightly to look up at him. My eyes wander to his lips, then to the slope of his neck where it meets his shoulders and disappears beneath his T-shirt.

Just when I think Jethro's about to say something, he reaches toward me. His finger touches my ear. "I'm guessing this was supposed to go on the canvas," he says, showing me a little blue paint he's wiped off.

We both laugh.

"There's something I wanted to ask you about," he says

now, suddenly serious again. "The Knock List, or whatever they're calling it."

Oh. I feel my heart sinking into a bottomless pit. "Yeah?"

Jethro puts his arms behind him and leans back against the wall, placing all his weight on his open fingers. "There was something on there," he says, "and when I saw it, I thought I was being paranoid. At first I didn't even really want to know, but I've been thinking about it all day, and maybe there's someone else, but I can't think of anyone else in school who'd search that right now. So I guess now I kinda need to know . . . if it was yours. To get it out of my head."

Of course I know exactly what he's talking about.

"*Avoid rebounding with a close friend?*" Jethro continues. "Was it about . . . me? Sorry if I'm being paranoid; it's just . . . no one else has broken up lately besides you . . ."

Breathing isn't coming easily. Staring into those eyes, I don't want to own up to it, but I can't bear to lie either. All I can manage is a weird half shrug.

Jethro inhales. My silence says it all. He drops his head and closes his eyes for a moment. Then opens them. "It sucks that Rad and Nik are being so hard on you," he says. "But they aren't the only ones who weren't psyched with the way things went down."

"I just . . . ," I whisper as some JV hockey players pass us. "I wanted to make sure you and I can be friends again. I don't want to . . . confuse things again. I know I wasn't so good about that last summer. And I guess I was worried that when I saw you today, now that Palmer and I broke up . . ."

"What?"

I take a breath. I hate myself for not being able to look him in the eye as I shrug again. It's that thing we've never acknowledged. That something-else part of our friendship that makes it so perfect *and* so complicated. It's the closest either of us has come to saying it out loud, and I can't do it.

Jethro's face is unreadable for a moment. Finally he says, "You might not believe this, but after three years of whatever this is . . . or isn't . . . I'm not sitting around on my ass waiting for you, Anna. I've hung out with other people."

Has he?

"Okay," I say.

"So anyway," he says, "don't worry about *confusing things* anymore. Not gonna happen." He shakes his head and turns to go. "You can leave the rebounding to your basketball-star ex."

It's the first time I can remember in four years of friendship that Jethro's walked away from me in the middle of a conversation.

"Here's a crazy idea. How about we do everything at this paper, like, a thousand times better this semester and show people that print journalism is alive and well?"

I'm standing in an overheated room on the top floor of Ewing, at the home of the *Xandria* offices. Junior year,

I did illustrations and cartoons for the newspaper, but I dropped it last semester. For the same reason I dropped everything else in my life. Now I need to show my most hard-ass friend that I'm serious about this comeback. So here I am after school, listening to Rad, early acceptee to Northwestern's prestigious school of journalism, Miss Editor in Chief, address her staff: comma-splice concerns, excessive use of the first-person singular, some fund-raiser happening a few weeks from now, at which attendance is mandatory, directions she wants to take the paper in this semester . . . The good news is, listening to my old friend talk—hanging on her every word in order to begin to prove myself again—is helping me forget about *avoid rebounding* and the super-awkward weirdness with Jethro. Kind of.

Rad's energy level picks up as she begins going off on "sleazebag upperclassmen" who have "zip minus diddly-squat passion" for journalism and are "barely coordinated enough to play Xbox" so can't go out for any teams and just want to pad their "weak-ass applications" for colleges, and how their "ass-wipe antics" will no longer be tolerated at the *Xandria*.

A few juniors exchange nervous looks.

"So," Rad says, looking at the crowd, "who's here to apply for staff positions?"

A sour smile clouds her face when she sees that mine is among the tentative hands hovering in the air. Folding her arms across her chest, she says, "So, Anna, you showed your little weasel, turncoat face after all. I didn't think you would."

People laugh awkwardly, unaware of how serious Rad is.

"And I'm to understand that you've seen the error of your faithless ways and that you wish to come crawling back to the *Xandria*?"

I nod. "Yeah . . . consider me one of thy faithful." Ugh, what am I even talking about? My guts twist from the room's attention.

Rad's smile turns smug. "Well. The *Xandria* is a beneficent institution. We'll take you back without making you endure a groveling session. At least not publicly."

Then Rad snaps her fingers, makes an *aw, shucks* face. "Oh, gee, I guess you should know that all the illustrator and cartoon spots are filled at the moment—darn. But you can point a camera too, right? And we need photographers!"

She stares right at me.

I can be as sorry as I want, but this is just downright cruel. Rad and I have spent *hours* talking about all the reasons why I don't like taking photographs. Hours discussing why it is I've spent the past two years doing paintings that make fun of selfies in the age of narcissism.

"I can take some pictures," I say with a level stare.

"I want our images to stand apart," she says. "High-quality, professional-looking shots of the athletes, not the athletes fuzzy in the background with some geek spectator flashing a Miley Cyrus tongue in front. You'll be covering the sports beat, by the way."

I know immediately: *Sports beat* doesn't mean I'll be covering girls' volleyball or coed fencing. I'll be covering boys' basketball and nothing but. She's going to make me go to every one of Palmer's remaining games.

So much for not seeing Palmer again.

But I can't back down now, in front of everyone.

"Sounds great." I flash a fake smile.

"Terrific," she says breezily. "We'll get you a press pass for Saturday's game, then." She holds my eye for one beat, two beats, three beats, then at last looks away. "Okay," she says to the group at large, "so what are the rest of you covering?"

4

"If there are six hundred students, and this 'glitch' on the app lasted forty minutes, then we're talking about a rate of three point seven five search queries per student, per hour, on average. Susan? Has our daughter ever asked us three point seven five questions in a *day*?"

My father leans back into his dining room chair with a smile, and Mom appears from the kitchen with a bread-basket and smile of her own. She has big, brown eyes that are perpetually wet and blinky, like a rabbit's. My parents both have accents—my dad's is Colombian, my mom's is Southern belle.

"Someone searched 'caffeine pregnancy'," Mom says. "Do you think they're *asking* if . . . caffeine causes pregnancy?"

"Also . . . what does *Netflix and chill* mean?" Dad asks with too much sincerity.

It's moments like these when I wish I had a sibling. Someone to suffer alongside when my parents are being utterly embarrassing. Welcome to Soler dinner hour, which would be canceled on *Funny or Die* before the first ad. Alejandro and Susan get how crappy it is that everything we searched at school this morning was being recorded by the school app, but the Knock List is still tonight's low-hanging teenage-comedy fruit. On a good day, when I'm in a good mood, their oh-so-witty banter can be a little bit funny. This is *not* one of those days.

"This chicken ain't gonna eat itself," Mom says, finally taking her seat.

Mom grew up in Georgia, and she's been on a Southern kick for the past year, and I'm not one to complain about mashed potatoes. Dad works at the embassy—he first came here as a diplomat twenty years ago—so he eats Colombian food all the time at lunch and wants anything but *ajiaco* at dinner.

"I was relieved to see how little of it was . . . of a pornographic nature," Dad says, wiping his mouth with a cloth napkin. "Idiotic, yes. But gives me hope for the future."

I scrape my fork across my plate. "Dad, it was nine in the morning on a Thursday. Who looks at porn then, anyway?"

"When I was in *colegio*, kids made out in the parking lot before the first bell."

"There was a parking lot in the eighteenth century?"

Dad snorts. "We put our horses and buggies there."

I have to say, I'm relieved my parents haven't asked me which searches were *mine*. This is the best thing about them: for all their jokes about high school drama, they don't get all up in my business very often. I know they've secretly read a thousand books about raising a child with SAD. Maybe it comes from that. They know I have Dr. Bechdel to talk to (and they think I still have friends), so they usually don't push. Dinner might be the best part of my day.

"Has anyone heard anything back from the colleges?" my mom asks lightly.

But I'm *really* not in the mood for that right now.

"Nope. Can I be excused?"

I promised myself I wouldn't check the Internet again until after dinner, and I barely made it through. Technically, part of the SAD management I've worked out with Dr. Bechdel is that I'm supposed to minimize my use of social media. I don't post anything anymore, and I have only anonymous accounts for the occasional lurking I still crave, like any normal person. Resisting Reddit for as many hours as I have is an accomplishment. So now I'll just . . . take a little peek.

Late this afternoon, someone copied all the Knock List searches into a Reddit thread, and users started trying to match them to people. By six p.m., almost three hundred of the searches were matched to specific kids at school. Some are obviously right—no one had any doubt that jazz saxophone player Ian MacKinnon was the one searching for *Ian MacKinnon Prep hot* or that Ashley Keup's idiot boyfriend, Steve, had done a search for *Keup family net worth*. It didn't take long for Reddit users to figure out that *Briana Texas Catfish* was Seth Habel's way of trying to make sense of the fact that his Twitter girlfriend, Briana, who asked him to send money to Houston last week, was a forty-five-year-old man in his underwear.

I'm lying on my bed now, laptop open. My bedroom is plastered with Lana Del Rey and René Magritte and Warhol posters. I haven't gotten around to redecorating, so my fourteen-year-old self is still in charge of the walls.

Page eight of the Knock List stares back at me.

No name has been assigned to either of my stupid search terms. Thank God.

One more thing. I go back to the first page, type *Anna Soler* into the search box.

Nothing.

Pages two and three: nothing.

Page four: *One hit.*

Wait. What? Oh God.

My eyes glaze over a little. When I'm able to focus again, I see my name next to the words *Silver Pines anonymous.*

But it's not even mine. I didn't write it!

Unfortunately, it won't be hard for people to believe I did.

I've had anxiety issues since I was little.

Separation anxiety from my mom in preschool lasted for more than a year, and anxieties about my skin in middle school kept me home for days at a time. Every few weeks my poor mom had to listen to twelve-year-old me wail and beg her not to make me go, had to hear how I was disgusting and ugly, how everyone was grossed out by me.

I made it through the beginning of Prep only by the grace of Nikki and Rad and Jethro. Having them as friends made life and social interactions tolerable for a while, but eventually even that wore off. Junior year I stopped making eye contact with people again, and my voice dropped to the same ragged whisper my parents knew too well.

Non-IRL interactions were even worse. Maintaining the Internet presence of a not wildly popular but also not totally losery high school girl was too much for me. I couldn't shake the feeling that everyone could tell that the facade I was trying to create was just that, a facade. Like all my followers could see me take fifteen selfies in my new bathing suit at the beach before posting one—not of me but of my shadow on the sand. Like they were all laughing at my insecurity and were right to.

Then there was the paranoia.

I knew that any post could be turned into a meme for the whole student body to feast on. Of course, everyone knew this. But I *really* knew it. Like, I couldn't get it out of my head that someone, somewhere, had screenshotted that photo of me at the *Game of Thrones* marathon—from three years ago!—in some *khaleesi*-style halter top I'd made out of a scarf, which Rad posted one night as a joke, taking it down only after I screamed at her three minutes after she posted it, an eon in Internet time.

That night was dark. I threw my phone across the room, and after an hour of thinking about what post could bring me back from the dead on social media, I started to feel like the walls, my bed, and everything else around me were trying to squeeze my body into a tiny little ball. My throat wouldn't open; I tried to get up from my bed, but it was completely impossible; half my vision went black; and then my face went numb. I felt like I was going to die, and I couldn't even call for help.

It was the worst panic attack I'd ever had.

The next day Dad tried to keep it light with one of his terrible jokes, and Mom held back her tears as they signed me in at the Silver Pines Clinic for Adolescents.

SP isn't exactly *One Flew Over the Cuckoo's Nest*. It's more like a year-round summer camp for kids who are "high strung" or suffer from narcissistic personality disorder. I talked to actual doctors with actual medical degrees, not just a guidance counselor. Getting a diagnosis was such a huge relief. It was confirmation that it wasn't all in my head. Like, I'm not just a freak! There's a *reason* I feel the way I do. They taught me how to manage it and also referred me to Dr. Bechdel, who continues to help with a long-term plan to overcome it.

Rad and Nikki and I had been inseparable since our Bratz dolls days, back before our interest in boys, before we knew about feminism, before our college application stress. They knew how I could get—how worked up and anxious and freaked out and weird. This was a whole new level of crazy, but Rad dealt with it mostly by reading me words of wisdom from Amber Rose's memoir, *How to Be a Bad Bitch*, over the phone. Nikki hand mailed cards with inspirational sayings. Haven and Andrew texted me videos (think capybaras in swimming pools) to cheer me up. None of them had any idea how to handle a chick with SAD, but they sure did try.

Jethro . . . sweet Jethro . . . he called every single day I was in there.

So, through some combination of my friends, group therapy, individual therapy, "freewriting" in my dream journal, meditation class, and Zoloft, I got better. Mostly. And that doesn't always happen. What I mean to say is, I was lucky.

Silver Pines anonymous. I lean back on my pillow and stare at the words.

I didn't exactly hide the fact that I'd gone to SP, but I didn't broadcast it either, and it seemed like people had been slowly forgetting it since last year. I thought dating Palmer had put the nail in the coffin. So much for that.

Suddenly, I realize that if I'm not the one who wrote it, *that query was someone else's.* It makes me sad to think that someone else at Prep is struggling enough to need a visit to Silver Pines.

The doorbell rings.

I look up from Reddit toward my bedroom door. My parents didn't say they were expecting anyone, and the days of Palmer showing up randomly are *waaay* over. I move to the window and peek outside.

Radhika stands on the front stoop, arms crossed.

"Hi," I say in a neutral voice as I close the front door behind me. It's freezing out, but Rad and I stay on the front porch, since there's no place in the house where we'll have privacy. "Are you here to torture me again? Honestly, I'm surprised you want to do it one on one. You seem to have so much fun doing it in public."

It's my best attempt at "whatever doesn't kill me." But Rad just laughs. Try as I might, we both know I can never be as razor sharp as she is.

Without a word, Rad reaches into the back pocket of her jeans and pulls out her American Spirits.

"You can't do that here," I tell her.

"Whatever. Your dad doesn't care. Everyone smokes in Bogotá."

"This is Fairfax, not Bogotá."

Rad lights a cigarette with a Bic with Marilyn Monroe making a kissy face on it.

"I like the cold," she says, picking a piece of tobacco off her tongue. "You'd think, being Indian, I'd be more into heat. But I like winter better."

"What're you doing here, Rad?"

"Where?"

"Here, at my house. What are you really doing? Because I think you're doing that thing that a cat does with a mouse it's already wounded—playing with the mouse until it gets bored and then killing it. So just, like, kill the mouse."

Rad looks amused. "Excuse me?"

"Go on. Tell me I'm a terrible friend again. I deserve it."

She blows out a plume of thick, pale smoke, watches it melt into the dark air—cream dissolving into coffee. "You're spineless and disloyal and don't seem to have the slightest grasp of girl code, but you're occasionally useful to me."

I can't help smiling. I missed her repartee. Even when it's insulting. I can tell she's straining not to laugh too.

"*Useful.* Wow. Okay. So where does that leave us?" I ask, plucking the cigarette from her fingers and taking a drag.

"On the way to a party," she says, like it's obvious.

I blink. "It's a school night."

She sighs, annoyed to have to explain things that I should already know. "No, it's a Thursday night. And in college, that's a weekend night. We're peacing out of high school in a few months, okay? We need to start practicing, getting our bodies adjusted to the new schedule. It's the first day of the last high school semester of your life. Something you in particular should be glad to celebrate, because it means that you won't have too many more chances to ruin every friendship you have."

I grimace at the ground. "Whose party?"

"Vanessa's."

I groan.

Rad, though, is having none of it. "You know Vanessa throws good ones. I got, like, a hundred snaps about it in the last hour. Lots of kegs, and her parents' McMansion is massive, and, best of all, they're never in it."

"Well, my parents are in my McHouse," I say. "And there's no way they're letting me leave it. I don't think they'll accept a *Thursday night is a weekend night in college-land* excuse."

"So sell them another one. Tell them you have to do something for the *Xandria*, that that's why I came over."

"I don't know," I say. "My mom will never buy it."

Rad hits me once, hard, on the upper arm.

"Ow!" I say, rubbing the spot.

"You're avoiding Palmer, aren't you?"

"No."

"Whatever. You'll be taking pictures of him all semester, so get used to it. Plus, Nikki will be there, and so will I, so you can begin your groveling program."

"Rad, I told you how sorry I am."

"Yeah, that won't do it. You're coming, and you're still on probation. One slipup, and you're done. Understand?"

"It's just . . . ," I say.

She shakes her head, uncomprehending. "What, bitchy face?"

"Did you see the Reddit?"

Rad *tsks*. "That Silver Pines thing? Who cares. It wasn't even you, was it?"

I like that she still knows me well enough to know. If only she knew how pathetic what I *really* searched is.

"Whatever, I'm so over the Knock List," Rad says. "Party. Now."

I don't want to face the masses, but getting an olive branch from my best friend in the world—how can I say no?

"You're powerless against me." Rad eyes my jeans and sweatshirt. "Change into a better outfit—you look gross. Also, you have to take your car. Nikki, Haven, Andrew, and Jethro are already coming in mine. I have to go pick them up."

I feel my eyes getting big in my head. "Haven? He's going? To Vanessa's?"

"You know Haven has a death wish." She chuckles, taking a final drag on her cigarette. "So, anyway, you can follow us there. Unless you want to sit on Jethro's lap."

Can she see how deeply I'm blushing in the dark?

"You guys looked like two goddamn peas at lunch," she continues, to my despair.

I lean back. Jethro obviously hasn't told anyone about our conversation. "He just wasn't making me his whipping girl."

"You and I both know he'd like to whip you any day."

"*Ew.*" I pause. "Just friends. I think."

"You think?"

"I mean, I think we're friends again. I hope we are."

"Keep it that way," Rad tells me. "You've messed up enough of us for one year."

I don't utter a word about her and Andrew. I can hear her response already, the same one I've heard a dozen times: *That's just sex, Anna, nothing else. Grow up.*

With the toe of her ankle boot, Rad kicks the cigarette butt off the porch and into the bushes. "And prepare to follow my commands over at Vanessa's. Think Theon Greyjoy. My wish is your *Yes, ma'am, I'm the shittiest friend, ma'am.*"

5

"I WASN'T EVEN IN THE COMP SCI LAB WHEN IT HAPPENED," Haven says. "They were working on some visualization tool and fishing for big data sets to throw into it, and they stumbled on the search terms. Then they just dumped it into an email. Sooo boring. It would've been much more spectacular if I'd been there."

Rad, Nikki, Andrew, and I are listening to Haven complain about how underwhelmed he is by the Knock List, which he's been doing all day, apparently. We're clustered on the front steps of Vanessa Eubanks's Spring Valley house—super new, super huge, and super tacky. Prep parents are a D.C. mix of spies, think tankers, too many lawyers to count, and soccer moms and dads, but a lot of us get some kind of financial aid. Not Vanessa's parents. Her dad is some kind of defense contractor who people say gets richer every time a foreign country is invaded. Which has made him pretty rich.

"My work has more flair," Haven continues. "More panache."

"Will all of you just shut up about the stupid leak?" Rad says. "Isn't there anything more interesting to talk about?"

"It *would* have been more interesting if I'd done it," Haven grumbles.

He's wearing a pair of *Lolita* sunglasses he must've found in the backseat of Rad's car (the lenses are heart shaped, the frames bright-red plastic), and he's turned his BYTE ME T-shirt inside out. It wouldn't fool a fourth grader, and, after the turkey-head spirit-squad announcement hack he perpetrated on Vanessa, I put our chances of making it inside with him somewhere in the Not Happening range.

Rad turns back to me. "Knock again," she says. *"Harder."*

Haven and Andrew laugh a little when I humbly do as the slave master tells me. Nikki doesn't—I guess she isn't quite ready to laugh about me yet. As we wait for my second, louder knock to be answered, the bass line of the song playing inside *thump-thump*s away, shaking the ground, sending vibrations up our legs.

"Is Jethro coming?" Nikki asks as we continue to wait.

Rad glances at me. "He said he can't stand Vanessa. I told him none of us can, which is why we're gonna drink all her booze."

I have a sinking feeling I know the real reason Jethro's not here.

Finally the front door opens, and the swell of noise and heat envelops us. "Hey there, come on in," says the drunk girl who answers. Actually, it's more like *heytherecomeonin*.

Vanessa's living room is a wreck. The furniture's been pushed carelessly to the walls to make space for a trio of kegs manned by Wallace Reid and a couple of the other basketball players. Bowls of M&M's and potato chips, some overturned, are scattered across various surfaces. Stereo equipment, balanced precariously on a window-sill, is blasting Rihanna. The cast of *A Midsummer Night's Dream* has gathered in the front of the living room, with Mattie Eizenberg at the center of the cluster. Nikki stares at the group longingly. Rad puts her hand on Nikki's back, pushing her forward.

"This is the night. Tell him you want to hear him do one of his amazing monologues," Rad whispers. "Upstairs."

"That's stupid," Nikki says as she stops short. "He'll never believe that."

"Please," Rad says. "He's an actor. He needs any and all validation."

Then Rad leans in and whispers something I can't hear to Nikki.

What I can hear is Nikki's response. "I can't do that!"

"You wanted to know how to make it happen tonight," Rad says loudly, jabbing her finger into Nikki's arm. "That's *how* you make it happen."

Once upon a friendship I would have stopped Rad from exerting pressure on Nikki about sex, but, since I'm on eggshells with her now, I stay quiet. Rad gives Nikki a final look, like, *Ignore me at your peril*, then summons

Andrew to come with her, heading for parts unknown—presumably dark, quiet parts where no one else is. Typical.

Neither Nikki nor I drink (I don't because of the vestigial habit to not mix meds and booze; Nikki doesn't because she's afraid of turning into her mom), and by silent mutual consent, we find a spot together by the back wall and sip from lukewarm cups of Diet Coke. For nearly a minute we watch the actors without a word.

It's the first time we've been together one-on-one in, well, months, and I'm not sure where to start. *How've you been?* feels way too shallow.

"You should go over," I say finally, trying to break the silence, trying to be a better friend. (Of course I don't want her to leave me where any random person could approach, but she needs to know where my priorities are.)

"Rad spent twenty minutes last night telling me that if I didn't find a way to get Mattie alone in a bed soon, she'd sleep with him first," Nikki blurts. I'm grateful for her confessional outburst. *Skip the small talk, let's dive back in*, she seems to be communicating. She's probably missed having someone to talk to about Rad too, I realize. The girls are thick as thieves, but they can definitely irritate each other.

"Just talk to him if you want to," I say. "You don't have to rush anything."

Nikki doesn't look at me. "I thought you didn't like Mattie."

I sigh. "Nikki, I think we all know that I'm the last person to be judging anyone's boy choices right now."

She shrugs. "Anyway. Those guys are all actors. I'm just on the crew."

51

"I saw you talking to Mattie this afternoon."

"That was different. That was, like, a mixed group with other random kids too. Not just the star Thesbos."

"You're a star set designer."

"Yeah," she says absently. "By the way . . . did you and Palmer . . ."

"Do it?"

"Yeah."

I laugh. We're officially back, up in each other's business.

Nikki smiles at me expectantly.

"Almost," I say.

"Well, that's good that you *didn't*, right?"

"I guess, yeah."

"Did you love him?"

I'd been purposefully avoiding talking about Palmer with her and Rad. But now, it actually feels good. I've been suppressing all these feelings and could really use some advice from my friends, aka not just Dr. Bechdel and my mom.

"I don't know," I say. "Maybe, for a while. But after we broke up, it didn't last. I just kinda felt stupid that I ever thought it was real. And that I screwed you guys over."

Nikki looks at me, then touches my arm. "I shouldn't have ignored you in the lounge, A. That was sucky."

"I get why you're mad at me."

Nikki shakes her head. "Rad really yelled at me after lunch, you know. She just . . . she plays the bitch, but I think you know she was actually pretty *hurt*."

"I know." I look at my hands.

She's about to say something else, but suddenly she falls silent. Across the room, Mattie is crooking a finger at her, giving her a sexy grin.

Nikki breathes in sharply, sucking in her stomach. "Wish me luck," she says.

Mattie welcomes her with a full-body hug, and the others move to make room for her at his side. Nikki smiles wide, which makes me smile.

But not for long. Because now here I am, standing alone at a party. My heart flutters, and I clutch my phone like it's my lifeline. I breathe deeply and make myself look busy—writing texts to nobody, fake-reading my Instagram. I know this party is a perfect scenario for my SAD to flare up. But sometimes I still can't believe how ridiculously uncomfortable I get being around other people. It's not that I don't *enjoy* socializing, under the exact right conditions; it's just that these aren't them.

Worst of all: when I do dare to look up from my phone, the first thing that catches my eye is Palmer. Vanessa is touching his arm and laughing wildly at something he's saying, which is absurd because Palmer is many things—very tall, sweet, sometimes even more vulnerable than I am—but he isn't all that . . . funny.

Palmer's also not as traditionally beautiful as Vanessa—he has big, deep-blue eyes and a rangy, midwestern build, just like his dad—but he and Vanessa are two members of the same tribe, probably both descended from Norse gods. And it looks like they're finally coming together. Their faces are close now, words moving back and forth between them fast and intensely, and Vanessa's got her hand on Palmer's arm.

I can't look away. It's not like I want to get back together with him. My friends are what matter now. So why can't I look away?

Maybe because I still don't get what happened.

This much I know: at the beginning of November, Palmer twisted his knee during a practice and tore a small part of his ACL. I rushed over to his house that night, of course, and I did my homework at his bedside every day after school for almost a month. Unfortunately, Palmer's knee wasn't healing as quickly as everyone hoped, and he got a little depressed. As soon it became clear that serious rehab was in order and that even serious rehab might not do the job, I could feel Palmer pulling away from me.

But I thought it was just a hiccup. I thought we'd get through it.

Unfortunately, I'd already abandoned my friends, and I had no one to talk to. No Rad or Nikki who could help me see the signs.

By Christmas, Palmer and I were over.

I barely ate for a week; I spooned with my pillow and cried in the dark. I thought that Palmer and I had had something special, that he *needed* me. I'd considered telling him we should just finally have sex, to get closer to him again. It's a dumb reason to decide to lose your virginity to someone, but that's what went through my puppy-love head.

Without my friends to set me straight, I was a complete and utter disaster. Overthinking led me into an emotional black hole.

When I finally talked to my mom, she cried with me. And in that weirdly comforting and absurd mother-daughter moment, something unexpected happened: I saw my thing with Palmer for what it was—a *thing*. A senior fling. What do they call it on those British costume dramas my mom watches? A *dalliance*. That's all. Palmer isn't my soul mate. He was my senior crush. I could get over it. And my mom—God bless her—definitely shouldn't be crying about my senior crush.

Vanessa cackles again at something Palmer's just said.

Move along, Anna. Stop staring. Everyone at this party knows exactly what you're thinking right now, and they're laughing at you. Mocking you. They all think you overstepped. That you dated up and you were lucky to get even a short ride on the popular bus. That you're hideous. That even your friends are too good for you.

I'm about to lose it when suddenly I remember: these are *negative thoughts*. And I know what I need to do. When I take a Dr. Bechdel–approved deep breath and look around, I see—there's no evidence of any of what I'm feeling. No one *is* looking at me. No one is laughing at me. As Dr. Bechdel would say, *What's the reality, Anna?*

The reality is that no one is mocking me. They're just ignoring me.

I walk over to the keg and pour myself a foamy beer. I'm six months post-Zoloft and haven't had a Xanax in more than eight weeks. I need something to loosen me up if I'm planning on staying. The Bud Light doesn't go down easy, but it goes down. Next, please! The beginning of my second cup goes down easier. Soon I'm starting to understand why people drink, melting comfortably into the wall behind the keg.

Vanessa stands and takes Palmer's hand. Before I can get in another gulp, they're walking off together. I track them with my eyes to the foot of the stairs. I know exactly what they're headed up to do. Everyone does. Maybe Nikki hit the nail on the head and it's good that Palmer and I only got to *almost*.

Maybe.

I'd made out with a couple of other guys before Palmer. But Palmer was my first real boyfriend, and physical stuff was so much easier with him than it had ever been with anyone else. Maybe *too* easy. The closer we got to having sex, the more I fell for him.

Just before his injury, Palmer and I were alone in his room. His parents were out, and we were on his bed, not lying down but not quite sitting up either. Frank Ocean album playing. Candles lit. One blew out when I took off Palmer's button-down. (I was a little hasty. What? He looked so good without a shirt on.)

Next thing I knew, he popped the question: should we *do it?*

When Palmer and I got together, I was a virgin as bad as Nikki. Palmer *wasn't* a virgin several times over, with several girls over. The difference in our experience bothered me, was always in the back of my mind, and it came to the front at that exact moment. So, to clarify: I wanted to have sex with him. I turned him down only because I was intimidated and scared and overwhelmed and taken off guard. In my fantasies, losing my virginity always happened without words, as if it were the easiest, most natural thing in the world—no blood or pain or awkwardness, no risk of him being disappointed or unsatisfied, of me not measuring up.

When he understood that I was signaling no, Palmer didn't get mad. He just kissed the top of my head and held me tighter. *No rush*, he said casually. But I can't help wondering: if I'd done what he wanted me to do and what *I'd* wanted me to do—let me be 100 percent clear about that—and had acted less like a 1950s prude and more like a normal girl born at the tail end of the twentieth century, would he have broken up with me so inexplicably?

"Yo. I didn't mean anything in the dining hall."

I look up from my beer, and I'm blinded by a gold Cuban chain necklace. It's draped around Wallace Reid's thick neck.

"Sometimes I get turnt and just kinda say stuff I don't mean," he says. "I'm not scamming on you. I was just joking."

I slowly count down from five, and finally I feel okay enough to say something he deserves. "Okay," I tell him, starting to edge away. "No harm, only a small foul." I want out of this conversation pronto.

Wallace knocks back his own nearly full beer, and somehow his throat seems to pulse only once, like he barely even has to swallow. "Dude, it's amazing. You and Palmer say the exact same things sometimes. Like, the same exact tone of—" He cuts himself off, realizing. "Sorry. Anna, I told him you two should keep hanging out."

"Maybe I'm not turnt enough," I deadpan.

"No, that was the problem. You were too cool."

This is the first time Wallace has ever said anything particularly nice to me that didn't seem like a come-on, and it catches me off guard. "What's that mean?" I ask.

Something creeps into his eyes that I don't get. Honestly, I didn't know he was capable of this kind of sincerity. "Whatever," Wallace says. "It's just—Palmer's got a lot on his mind. It's not about you."

"No. Apparently it's about *Vanessa*. I saw them heading upstairs," I say, emboldened from chugging two beers in a row.

He shrugs. "Nah. Vanessa just—Palmer doesn't care what she thinks of him. He's just, ya know, under a lotta pressure from all sides. Kid's gotta let it out somewhere."

I don't understand. *Pressure from all sides?*

"You," a shrill voice hisses from a few feet behind us. "You have the balls to show up at my house?"

Wallace and I turn. I don't see Palmer anywhere, but Vanessa is standing face to face with Haven, right next to us.

"Wait, is this not Selena Gomez's crib?" Haven says. "Shit, wrong party."

People start laughing.

Vanessa throws her gin and tonic in Haven's face.

"Oh wow," Haven says, wiping liquid off his chin. "I didn't know people did that IRL. Classy."

"I should slap you into next week."

Haven smiles wide as more people squeeze toward us. "It's @theVanessaeubanks, right? PerfectlyVanessa@gmail? And oh, wait, Vantastic00 on Snapchat, right?"

What he's saying is: *Prepare to be trolled.*

I love watching Haven be badass, but I do *not* like standing near a scene. I don't want to be pulled in, I don't want to be looked at. I start to back away. Kids are giggling and yelling things, and now practically the whole party is moving toward the action. Everyone is waiting for something nasty and vicious and fun to happen.

Fight, fight, fight, some say from behind me.

Before I can get away, I'm surrounded on all sides.

My forehead starts to sweat. The gulp of beer left in my cup begins to slosh back and forth as my hands tremble. Then comes the feeling I remember too well from junior year, the palpitations—what doctors call it when your heart feels like it's dancing to the beat of a drummer with no rhythm. Body heat and beer breath and screechy voices get louder and louder as Vanessa and Haven yell at each other. I don't really hear their words clearly; my eyes swing back and forth without focusing on anything. I try to take in air but can't. It won't enter my lungs, stops prematurely. The hysteria builds inside me, and I want to run out. But I can't move. It's like my mind is going at light speed and my body—stimulated as it is—won't go anywhere.

From the corner of my eye, I see someone pushing his way through the crush of bodies.

Jethro?

When did he get here?

As he reaches me, I say through gritted teeth, "Can you please get me out of here?" He nods and swiftly guides me out a glass door, into the backyard and bracing cold.

"Focus on your breath," he says. "Inhale, exhale. Inhale, exhale."

Jethro's voice is soothing, and the sensations of him standing near me—the smell of him, the warmth that comes off his skin—are so comforting that I take just a little longer to get my breath back than is strictly necessary. He doesn't seem to mind.

He helps me over to a stone wall that looks out onto a man-made pond, iced over at the moment. "You're freezing," Jethro says, frowning at the bumps that have broken out all over my exposed arms. "Stay here," he says. "I'll be back in a minute."

It takes him closer to three than one, but he returns with two coats, neither of which belongs to us. He throws the smaller one over my shoulders. It's fur, so thick that when I reach up to touch it, my hand sinks in up to my wrist.

Jethro laughs as he sits down beside me. "I swiped them from the front hall closet. Vanessa's mom probably had some endangered species skinned to make it." Then he holds his arm up: an even bigger fur coat. "Who knew Vanessa's dad was a Kardashian?"

For the moment, it feels like everything that happened in the art lab is gone. I hope it's gone forever.

Jethro looks around. "Know what would be better than this place?"

I smile back at him. "Tell me."

He lifts a single finger in the air, conjuring something. "Mui Ne Beach. Vietnam. The winds blow hard and steady every afternoon, so people come from all over the world to go kiteboarding. We take lessons, camp on the beach at night, stay until we're kick-ass, eat pho until we have to undo the first buttons on our jeans."

I breathe in and out. "What if we went *sandboarding* instead? There's an oasis in the desert in Peru. Huacachina, I think it's called. They have these dunes that rise above the lake, and you can ride all the way down to the bottom."

"*Yeah,*" he says, the moon flickering in his eyes. "That's way better. Peru."

"Thanks for staying with me out here," I tell him. "And, J, can we just talk about how awkward our conversation outside the art lab was for a sec . . . ?"

"Forget it," Jethro says. "Never happened."

I don't know if he believes that, but right now I couldn't be happier to hear it.

"Do you wanna get out of here?" he asks.

"Are you kidding me? *Yes,*" I say. "But we can't. At least I can't."

"Why not?"

"Because I just chugged two beers! Now I'm stuck here until the sun comes up or I sober up. Whichever comes first."

"Gimme your keys. I'll drive."

"Uh-uh. I don't want to get drunk driven any more than I want to drunk drive."

"I'm the most sober person at this party."

"That's not saying much."

"Good point. But I'm totally sober."

I point to his beer cup.

"Been nursing this all night," Jethro says. "While I was looking for you."

"Then what are we still doing here?"

6

I'VE ALWAYS LIKED BEING DRIVEN MORE THAN DRIVING. NOTHING like sitting in the passenger seat and staring out the window, especially in a dreamy beer haze. The cold glass on my forehead feels amazing as I watch the streetlights flicker by.

Jethro's good behind the wheel—skillful, fast without being reckless. He negotiates tight turns, manipulates the steering wheel with deft little flicks of the wrist. I guess we're just tooling around, going no place in particular, passing time.

I feel kind of . . . great. It's been a long time since I could honestly say that.

A few minutes later, we enter Old Town Alexandria. The streets are well lit but mostly empty. My favorite diner isn't far away (and is probably the only place open at this hour), but just as I'm about to suggest a rocky-road shake, I see the Torpedo Factory Art Center coming up on

the right, lit up in bright contrast to the long-closed buildings around it.

"Whoa," I say. Jethro slows and turns into the parking
lot. "It's open this late?"

Jethro shrugs. "Not to the public, but has that ever
stopped us before?"

This massive building was once an *actual* torpedo factory. During World War II, I think. At some point the navy
decided to not build bombs so close to our nation's capital,
and it eventually became a home for more than one hundred artists, each with their own individual studio. Make
art, not war—kinda great, right?

"Come on," Jethro says, unbuckling his seat belt. "Let's
paint this town . . . I dunno . . . azure red."

"Azure is blue."

"That's what I said."

A bubble of happiness fills my chest as we head from
the far corner of the parking lot toward the front entrance
of the steel-and-glass building.

"Remember last time we were here?" he asks, almost
shyly.

"Yeah!" I say too loudly, then lower my voice. "It was
right after I got back from Silver Pines. You got that early
viewing for us. There were only, like, ten other people."

"I have my VIP ways," he says in a mock-fancy voice.

"No way could I have handled all those crowds after
SP. And B. J. Anderson? Her watercolors changed my life.
Honestly, J, it made me want to be a better artist myself.
I don't think I'd be applying to RISD if it hadn't been for
that day."

Jethro's grinning. "I had fun too, A."

We've stumbled into the lingering end of some exhibition's glamorous opening reception. The show features massive oil paintings, all of which are in the Rothko colorfield style. The crowd appears to have mostly thinned out; twenty or so folks stand around a table with plates of hors d'oeuvres and half-empty bottles of wine, more interested in conversation than in looking at the art. In Vanessa's parents' fur coats, we fit in surprisingly well, but I notice an older couple looking our way.

"They're probably just thrilled that anyone under the age of fifty cares about art," Jethro mutters to me as he grabs my hand. "Come on, come with me."

Jethro confidently leads us out of the lobby, into a long hallway, glancing around casually like he's the property manager doing some routine inspection. A step behind him, I can't help but watch each movement he makes, notice the curve of muscle along the backs of his tan arms, the way his jeans fit his narrow waist, how his legs bow out ever so slightly. As we turn a corner and he looks over his shoulder at me, those green eyes catch the overhead lights just right.

I clap a hand over my mouth to keep from squealing. The lights are dim, but all the individual artists' studios are still lit, their amazing work on just the other side of large windows: our own private gallery. It's so beautiful.

"What if someone sees us?" I whisper as I bounce from one foot to the other.

"Pretend you're an art student here if anyone asks," Jethro tells me. "Give 'em some more of that fancy azure talk."

He winks as he says it. He knows that if someone spoke to us or questioned our being here, I'd just blurt an apology and bolt for the door. Jethro would be in charge of any and all unexpected human interaction. But I still love when he pretends, when he makes me feel like I could easily be part of his scheme.

We peer into each artist's studio one at a time, taking in all kinds of pieces in various states of progress. A rounded bronze sculpture like a Brancusi glows gold through the glass of one. And behind and above it hangs a geometrically pleasing painting of migratory geese flying in a V.

"The strokes are so beautiful," I say, pointing. "Do you see how she just dips the tip of the brush into the oil, then dusts the canvas? Really makes those birds fly."

"I knew you'd hate it back here," Jethro says with a smile. He bumps my shoulder with his, and a flurry of butterflies is released in my stomach.

We make our way to the second floor. I'm not sure if it's the dramatic light or the echoes in the stairwell, but I feel like Jethro and I are in a dream. Or a music video. Never in a million years did I think I'd get this back—let alone so soon. We're on one of our old adventures, a Jethro and Anna Special.

I feel so lucky for this moment. It's kind of weird to feel lucky for something *while* it's still happening, in the present. When I glance back and he looks up at me, I know Jethro can feel it too. It's . . . what's that SAT word? *Palpable*.

At the top of the stairs, I wait for Jethro to fall into

66

step beside me. His knuckles brush against mine so lightly, I might not have even noticed except for the thrill of electricity it sends up my arm. I'm about to brazenly (drunkenly) grab his hand when a pair of paintings grabs my attention.

"This is Diane Tesler!" I yell-whisper, putting my face against the glass door to get a closer look.

Jethro puts his head next to mine. "Who is she?"

"Uh, only the greatest living painter in driving distance." I bonk his head gently for emphasis. "I mean . . . how many painters can make an abandoned truck and an antique toy look like *that?*"

He peers through the glass, trying to see what I see. His face glows in the dim light. In his green eyes, I can see the tiny flecks now. Any half-decent artist would call them coyote brown. They glint with something burning behind them that I'm sure I can feel dancing across my shoulders, making my breath a little shakier. It's a rare and exquisite kind of panic unfolding in me right now that feels . . . *so good*.

I lower my eyes. I'm so aware of how close our faces are, of the warmth coming off his skin.

"Anna," Jethro whispers. His voice sounds careful.

The word *rebound* pops up in my head, surrounded by question marks and teardrop emojis. I swat it out of my head like a fruit fly. My hand reaches for him almost reflexively, and his fingers slip between my own. My heart hammers behind my ribs.

What am I *doing?*

He inches a step closer.

I can't look up. So I bury my head in his chest and breathe him in. Tide detergent and delicious boy smell. What is that magical smell? He feels so solid, and I can hear his heart racing with mine.

"I missed you," I whisper to his T-shirt.

I hear his breath catch and then the smile in his voice when he says, "I know. I'm pretty awesome."

With a laugh, I whack his chest with my fist. "I know."

Jethro slides a hand along my neck, his fingers catching in my hair, sending a bolt of lightning down my spine.

Suddenly, the beam from a flashlight bobs around the corner, followed by the static of a security guard's walkie-talkie.

I feel my eyes bulge in my head, very real panic ready to set in, but Jethro just grins, grabs my hand, and pulls me down the hallway.

We race from the Torpedo Factory, sprinting past the last few reception guests and across the dim parking lot, my boots kicking against the Eubankses' fur coat. The cold air bites my flushed cheeks as we catch our breath between bouts of laughter.

"Whew! Close one," Jethro says. His wide smile makes his eyes crinkle, and I want to run my fingers through his wild, Hemsworthian hair.

I fumble for my keys. My teeth clack loudly. Jethro moves to stand square in front of me and rubs my furry arms. I forget what I'm doing as I look up at him. His face is bright from our run and the winter air; his breath puffs out around me in the thick darkness.

I click the button to unlock the car, but neither one of us moves.

Without a second thought, I push myself up on my toes to close the space between us and press my lips against his once, quickly.

He looks at me, stunned, and blinks. I'm shaking, but I'm not sure it's the cold anymore. I feel energized and reckless and want him so badly—

I lean in again.

This time Jethro moves forward and kisses me back, hard. His lips move against mine—slow and searching at first, then greedily, hungrily, like he never wants to stop.

I wrap my arms around his neck and lean back against the car, letting him pin me there. His whole body presses against mine, the weight of it lighting my nerves, and somehow it's not close enough. I don't think he could ever be close enough.

I kiss him until I'm gasping. His mouth moves down my jaw and my neck. I wind my fingers in his shirt, clutching his shoulders as his teeth graze the curve of my ear.

Something like a groan vibrates deep in Jethro's throat.

My lips find his again, desperate and wild, as he presses me harder against the car and pulls open the door.

I lean back and fall, stolen fur first, onto the backseat, pulling Jethro with me. My hands search for the warm skin at the bottom of his T-shirt.

He shudders, says against my mouth, "Your hands are freezing," but his words are as wobbly as mine get when I'm nervous.

I reply by pulling his fur off, then his shirt over his head. He snakes his arms around me and kisses me deeply.

7

WHEN MY ALARM GOES OFF, I'M POSITIVE THERE'S BEEN SOME mistake. There's no way it's already 6:30 a.m. But when I turn to my bedside table, the numbers 6, 3, and 0 are flashing at me in demonic red. Before I can groan, a thought pops into my head that crowds out all the rest.

I lost my virginity a few hours ago. To one of my best friends.

Maybe it's the wicked hangover I have right now that's overwhelming every other physical sensation, but I don't feel any different. No more like a woman than I did yesterday. After basically five years of thinking about sex in one way or another every day—wondering what it would be like, what I would feel like after—everything seems pretty much the same. It was a little painful at the beginning last night, but then it got better fast. I can't feel anything different down there now, like I always heard you do. He

71

used a condom, and it didn't last *that* long, but I don't really know how long it was supposed to last anyway.

Wiping drool from my cheek, I struggle through tangled blankets and the throbbing in my head to sit up. The bit of sun seeping between the drawn curtains hurts my eyes. My tongue is a dried-out crust. I slap the clock and let autopilot take me to the bathroom, turn on the shower. The one other time I've been hungover in my life was at a wedding in Bogotá when I was fourteen, when my older cousins got this unsuspecting half gringa lit on *canelazo*. I feel a billion times worse today.

Scalding water crashes down, steam clouding my vision, and the night slowly comes back to me. I feel a weird detachment from the specific events, but I remember everything in detail—drinking those beers, Palmer and Vanessa, then Haven and Vanessa, the panic attack, Jethro, the Torpedo Factory, the car, the condom.

The sex.

I had sex with Jethro.

I whisper it out loud several times into the hiss of the running water, but that doesn't make it seem any more real. It happened. I know it did. I was there. I . . . started it. He asked me half a dozen times, every step of the way, if I was ready. If I thought it was a good idea. But I didn't want to think. My whole life feels like one big thinkfest. All I wanted, for once, was to feel. To throw thinking to the curb.

I smush my forehead against the cool tile while the hot water runs off my nose, over my squeezed-shut eyes. My brain feels like a cracked-open egg sloshing around in my skull. And in my stomach. I gag and force the feeling back down, turn off the water. The bathroom begins to cool. I breathe deeply through my nose, hold it, let it out slooowly.

It's been almost two weeks since Palmer and I broke up. Who am I?

I went from barely having been kissed to having a serious boyfriend, breaking up, and now losing my virginity in less than six months.

As I turn off the shower spigot, the word *rebound* flashes through my head like it's on some sign held up by a game-show host.

I chug a glass of water, and then another. Hydration kills hangovers, I remember Rad saying once. I throw on my least high-maintenance outfit—my body needs some TLC. A long-sleeved tee and my reliable overalls. Then I stumble over to my bedside table and grab my phone. I unlock it with my thumb and see there's one new text. A long one.

From Jethro.

Certain phrases instantly leap out at me, almost knocking me over:

ever since sophomore year
even better next time
greatest night of my life
nothing else matters now

Oh God. No. *What?*

My mind races. It's a sweet, mushy, *flattering* message. It does make my insides feel like butterflies just moved in and will be living there forever. But—how can he be so sure about this? What happened to the great, casual hookup culture that the millennials before us invented? I know Jethro's had sex a couple of times before too, so it's not even his first! And it's senior year, for God's sake!

I love Jethro. I really do. As a friend, and maybe . . . maybe it could be more. Maybe it *is* more. Maybe it's *always* been more.

But!

This text is *intense*. Do I have to respond right away? I'm not *at all* sure what to say. Here are a few things I *am* sure of, though:

1. I have never, in my entire life, been more desperate for that kind of attention or affection. Which means I can't really be trusted to make rational decisions about boys. Even ones I love in some way or another.
2. Jethro doesn't want to be a rebound. He told me that himself just yesterday, and Jesus, I did it anyway, which he must see as proof that I am *as totally sure about this as he is,* 'cause what kind of friend would do that to him unless she was sure?
3. Rad said not to screw anything else up. How many more strikes till I'm out?

I stare at the phone screen like it holds a key to this enormous new problem I've just created in my life. The more times I reread his message, the more I realize last night was too far, too fast.

Jethro's always been there for me. He's completely adorable; he's always loved me, never abandoned me, always made me smile no matter what's wrong in my life. He knows all the worst parts of me, and maybe that's a good thing, after all, *not* something to avoid. And yet I know one thing for certain: Jethro's friendship is too important to me to let it get messed up.

A knock on my door makes my head feel like it's exploding with every knuckle rap. "Anna," my dad says from the other side, his voice sharp with concern, "your mother and I went to sleep at eleven. You still weren't home. I called and you didn't answer."

"I told you, Dad, I was shooting for the paper."

"You shouldn't have screened my calls."

Yeah, well, I shouldn't have done a lot of things.

"Sorry, Dad!" I call out, and grab my backpack.

I turn my hand into a visor as I walk through the Prep hallways between classes because the fluorescent lights are hella bright. By lunch, not one academic fact has penetrated the fog of my pounding headache. Still, fortunately, I have managed to have zero encounters with friends or more-than-friends, or ex-friends or ex-more-than-friends.

I have fifth period free, so I head out to the parking lot to nap in my car, which is, admittedly, a pretty low depth.

"ANNA!"

Rad's right hand is behind her back. A thin tendril of smoke rises above her head like she's sprouted a single devil's horn. Rad often sneaks a smoke in the parking lot during lunch. If all my synapses had been firing, I'd have gone somewhere else.

"Heyyy," I say. But as the word escapes my mouth, I realize there's about ten times too much enthusiasm. She'll see right through it.

"Been looking for you," Rad says, eyeing me skeptically. "I was thinking you could do one of my calc problem sets as your punishment for today."

"Rad, not now. I'm, like, really hungover. . . ."

"Were you that drunk at the party?"

"Nothing too crazy . . ." I trail off. And I pray she'll leave it at that.

She runs an appraising eye over my face, my clothes. "You're making Lindsay Lohan look like Kate Middleton today," she says, not mean, just matter-of-fact. "You must've had a *really* good time last night."

"Yeah, it was okay. Thanks for inviting me."

"Have you seen Nikki?"

"No. Why? She okay?"

"She's more than okay. Don't worry, she'll find you. Which is more than I could say for *you* last night. You disappeared after the Eubanks-Dodd smackdown."

"Oh," I say cautiously, trying not to lie. I seriously doubt Jethro would ever say anything to the girls about what happened. "I got panicky. Had to get out. I thought you were off with Andrew, anyway."

I don't know if Rad even knows Jethro showed up at the party. But what I've decided is that, while I won't lie if she or Nikki asks me a direct question about what happened (honesty equals part one of getting your friends back), I'm not going to volunteer anything either. Not yet, anyway. Of course I want to tell her that I'm no longer looking over the wall of virginity from the other side. I know that she of all people will be proud. Impressed, even. Of course I want to spill my guts and confess and ask her how to handle Jethro now. But I have to figure out what the hell to *do* with these kinda-sorta feelings.

Fortunately, Nikki comes jogging up to us and saves me from having to talk about last night anymore. She has a huge smile on her face.

"Did you tell her?" she asks Rad, breathless.

I squint. "Tell me what?"

Rad shakes her head. "She hasn't done nearly enough penance yet today."

Nikki: "Come on, Rad."

She looks at me warily. "*Fine*. We will show Anna that we are real friends, that we aren't monsters, like she is."

Nikki turns to me with a smile. "I was with Mattie last night!" she squeals.

"Last night?" I say. "You hooked up?"

"Oh, it was so much more than hooking up, Anna," she says. "It was like . . . a Nicholas Sparks movie, except not cheesy. He told me how much he likes me and was glad I joined the crew, and he thinks I'm hot and talented, and then he kissed me." She pulls down the neck of her shirt to reveal a hickey. "Then," she continues excitedly, "after Vanessa kicked the crap out of Haven, we went out to his car, and . . ." Nikki's eyes dance from Rad's face to mine, back to Rad's. "Well, I lost it."

I'm trying to process what she's saying.

"Wait. You mean . . . *It* with a capital *I*?"

Nikki nods.

Oh wow. Big night last night. Two-for-one special at the V-card incinerator. I lost *It* with a capital *I* in a haze of confused feelings and nostalgia and ill-timed decision making, and Nikki got her fairy-tale First Time.

"Our little girl, gone wild," Rad says.

I know I have to say something. Now. "How do you feel?" I ask.

Nikki, in a hushed voice: "It was perfect. Well, actually, it really, really hurt. Why didn't you tell me it hurt so much, Rad?" She smacks Rad's arm. "Anyway, it was amazing being with Mattie, and now I'm just thinking . . . are we a couple now? How do I ask him without sounding desperate or like a complete clueless dork?"

"Whoa, eager beaver," Rad says. She points at Nikki's crotch. "Or whatever you have down there these days. I love a good Sparks flick, but Zac Efron doesn't just walk into your life, take your V-card, and love you forever and ever, amen, in real life."

Nikki frowns. "Mattie's more of a Ryan Gosling, I think, but—"

"Nik, focus. Take one of Anna's weird deep breaths," Rad says. I look at the sky. Oof, that sun is too much for my headache. Rad is still going strong. "Play it cool, like it's no big deal. Less Sparks, more . . . Amber Rose. Besides, and most importantly, it's senior spring. Hos before Bromeos," Rad says, pointing to me. "Be careful or you'll end up in the sixth circle of hell with this one."

Nikki says, "Don't worry. No matter what happens, you guys always come first."

Rad shakes her head, nods at me. "That's what she used to say. Look how that turned out."

Nikki turns to me reassuringly. "It turned out okay in the end. Here we all are."

"Thanks, Nik."

"Speaking of people with too much mercy for you in their heart," Rad says, clearly bored with this love-fest, "I saw Jethro in third. He was, like, acting super hyper. It was weird. Like he was high or something, he was so happy. I think Andrew must've gotten some really strong stuff. Do you know what his deal is?"

I know Jethro wasn't high; he rarely smokes, and he definitely doesn't do it at school. But I know exactly why he was bouncing off the third-period walls.

"Not a clue," I tell them.

So much for honesty.

Friday-afternoon chapel is one of Prep's oldest traditions, dating back more than a hundred years. Because it's the twenty-first century and we live in secular times, the ritual is stripped of most religious implications, even though it takes place in a large, vaulting space full of pews and kneelers and stained-glass windows depicting famous scenes from the Bible, with a Jared Leto–looking Jesus hanging from a cross. I sit toward the back with Rad and Nikki, whose face is stuck in a permanent, postcoital smile.

Headmaster Nichols's address is about the Knock List. He talks confusingly about how an upgrade to the school's app, Prep for Today, caused yesterday's glitch, with some techie mumbo jumbo about "cloud vendors," "mainframe terminals," and something else no one cares about.

Rad points with her chin to the other side of the chapel. Haven, head tipped back against the pew, Adam's apple jutting out, is dead asleep. Next to him, Andrew stares off into space. Then, on the other side of Andrew, farthest from us, I see Jethro for the first time. He must have slipped in late.

My breath quickens at the sight of him. I can't tell if it's because I'm excited to see him or if it's because I'm terrified to talk to him. Either way . . . it's going to be awkward. Maybe I can avoid him all day. Or forever? How are you supposed to *act* around someone you've had *sex* with? I wish I could ask Rad without having to actually tell her anything about my situation. But I'm pretty sure an *I have this friend* question isn't going to cut it. He runs a hand through his hair, and a thrill ripples through my stomach as I flash back to those fingers in my hair, to kissing in the parking lot.

Damn it.

"Every word you type and text, every pic you snap and chat, is recorded somewhere on the Internet," Nichols continues booming. "Your generation is the first to have your entire lives digitized, and it's up to you to manage what gets recorded forever. You never know when it will come back to haunt you. Seniors, especially, should take great care, as colleges are most certainly watching . . ."

Rad scoffs, hisses in my ear, "I'm sorry, did he say *we* need to be more responsible? *He's* the one who didn't know Big Brother was recording us!"

I bump fists with her and tune out the rest of Nichols's speech.

All I want is to go home and crawl into bed, close my eyes, and keep them closed for fifteen hours or so.

Finally, chapel is over, and we're up and filing out along with everyone else when I feel someone's hand on my arm. "Hey," Jethro says, tugging lightly. "Got a minute?"

So this is going to go down way sooner than I had hoped. *How* did he get over here so fast? "Sure! Yeah!" I say, my voice unrecognizably high pitched.

Jethro leads me down a short hall and into a little out-of-sight nook. This isn't the place I imagined talking to him. In my mind it was at his house or somewhere else private. Now the delicious smell of him is pulling me back to the Torpedo Factory again, and it's hard for me to focus.

We stare each other in silence for a few seconds, then suddenly burst out laughing at the awkwardness. Jethro reaches out and takes my hand. For a split second I wonder whether he's going to kiss me. For part of that split second, I want him to.

"My text was too much. I know," he says. "I was just—"

"No," I say too quickly. "It was totally fine."

"Fine?" Jethro smiles. "How bad did it make you freak out? Like, was it better or worse than when Snape killed Dumbledore?"

I take a deep breath. "Last night was . . . really nice," I say carefully.

He nods. "It was. But we can take it slow. There's no rush. And if you wind up going to RISD, we're only gonna be an hour away from each other next year."

Next year?

As he talks about buses that run between Providence and Boston, where he'll be at MIT, my mind races. I haven't even gotten *into* RISD yet! He's already thinking about next year? Next year—when we're supposed to be finding ourselves at college, making new friends, getting out of Virginia and not looking back? This is getting real . . . fast.

"You okay, A?" he asks me now.

As I inhale and exhale, I know one thing for sure—I can't trust my feelings for him right now, and I don't want to hurt him more. I slowly pull back my hand from his, and the first cracks of worry creep across his face. Like he already knows what's coming.

"I care about you so much," I say, gaining control over my wobbly voice. "But . . . I don't know that this is the right time for us."

Jethro looks at me, processing. "You don't know that. What about *last night?*"

I feel heavy. The depth of my feelings for him, the connection we have, makes every word harder to say than the last. "It was amazing," I say. "But, I mean, I just got dumped. And we don't know what's happening next year. Plus, we haven't talked in months, and now we're just hooking up without even thinking about it?"

Jethro closes his eyes. Then opens them again. Finally

82

he says, "We've known each other *years*, Anna. I know you've felt it. You *can't* deny there's something here. . . ."

I hate being so indecisive when he's so sure about what he wants. But I can't stand here in front of him and tell him I want to start a relationship right now either, when so much is up in the air for me.

"I know. I know," I say. "It's . . . just . . . I'm really just trying to figure it out."

"*Wait*," Jethro says now, opening his eyes wide. "Is this about *Palmer*?"

The question catches me off guard. "What?"

"Is it *Palmer*? Are you still in love with him, Anna?" Sadness and anger are creeping into his voice. "Am I just your goddamn rebound?"

I swallow hard. "No. I don't know. But I mean, it has only been a couple of weeks since he and I broke up—you know that."

"And you're not over him, are you?"

"I . . . I guess I don't know what I am."

The look on Jethro's face now hurts me. Like, a knife stabbing and twisting into me. I have to focus harder than I ever have to keep the tears out of my eyes.

"I'm sorry," I manage to whisper.

Jethro says just two words. "*Fuck*, Anna."

He slides past me—careful, I notice sadly, not to touch me—then walks quickly down the hallway. I call his name, but he doesn't look back.

When he turns the corner, I let the tears come.

8

THERE IS A REASON WHY PAINTINGS ARE BETTER THAN PHOTOS. It's because they are closer to true human vision. You're probably saying *Photos don't miss anything; they capture every detail.* But no lens can ever match the human eye. A painter's brush can actually come closer to that truth than any SLR, which is part of why I avoid cameras like the plague. Of course, Rad knew all this when she assigned me the job of taking pictures of the basketball team. Payback's a bitch.

I get to the gym early to practice with the camera, but after a few minutes of fiddling with shutter speed, I give up. Automatic mode will do. My *Xandria* pass means I get one of the best seats in the house for the basketball game: smack-dab in the middle of the front row of the press box, which is just below the scoreboard.

I've been thinking about Jethro for almost every minute I've been awake during the past two days. Feeling his body up against mine. But now I've messed everything up. I made my bed, and I have to lie in it alone. Totally alone.

Suddenly, taking photos of Palmer and the basketball team feels like sweet relief from thinking about Jethro. (Yeah, yeah, I see the irony.)

Just then, I see Rad cutting through the crowd like a Prep mom late for CrossFit, holding my press pass out like a hot venti latte. Nikki's up behind her, waving.

"Hey, girl," Nikki greets me.

"Don't let your sweaty palms drop that Nikon, Soler," Rad says, cutting straight to the chase. "The *Xandria* can't afford to replace it."

"Has anyone seen Mattie?" asks Nikki, blowing a bubble with her gum.

"No," I say, "but I haven't been looking. You talk to him?"

Nikki shakes her head miserably. "He hasn't said anything to me at all. He hasn't called or texted since last night. I mean, I saw him at chapel yesterday, and so I texted him afterward but I didn't hear back until, like, ten p.m."

"And have you texted him today?"

"Twice. And sent him a DM, but that was just a link to something on BuzzFeed." Now she looks a little sheepish. "And . . . I called him."

"Just once?" I ask.

"I left two voice mails. The first one got messed up."

Rad shakes her head. "A call is like the equivalent of *ten* texts. Don't make me confiscate your phone. No more until you hear back from him, Cinderella."

I still haven't said a word to either of them about Jethro. And apparently he's also nursing his own romantic hangover alone; not even the boys have said a word about him except to casually mention he's been home sick.

The Prep warm-up theme song comes on—Eminem's "Lose Yourself." Rad starts to lead Nikki toward their seats in the bleachers and points me toward the press box. Over her shoulder, Rad says, "Slim Shady is speaking to you: *This opportunity comes once in a lifetime.* I.E., don't disappoint me."

"Are you seriously quoting Eminem, Rad?" Nikki laughs as they walk away.

When I'm alone again, I start snapping pictures of the crowd. The gym is packed tonight—it always is for home games. But there's a special excitement in the air. This is Palmer's first game back from his injury. Everyone wants to know: Is he the same player? Does he have the same speed and spring and pop?

Recruiters from major colleges have been calling Palmer since he was a freshman. But when he stepped on his teammate's foot at the beginning of November—twelve days before *early* National Letter of Intent Day—he twisted his knee and was carried off the court. The following week, word got out that he had a ligament tear, and several of those schools, including Duke, began to back off.

I could only imagine how it really made him feel. *Imagine* is what I had to do, because he refused to talk about it. Except for once, when I mentioned the upcoming regular National Letter of Intent Day, in April. I asked if he was going wait till then to sign with a school, to see if Duke would start sniffing around again after he healed. That day, Palmer referred to himself as "damaged goods" with a bitter laugh and then shut down. Soon we started seeing each other less, Palmer insisting that he was fine and that he just needed to focus on his recovery. I tried to respect his space and pretended I was okay with being walled off, but it hurt.

Then, on the Friday before holiday break, I felt a tingle of excitement when Palmer texted me. His message was brief: *Can we get coffee tomorrow? Killer ESP @ 2?* I just knew he was going to apologize for acting cold and moody lately. I'd forgive him. Of course I would. If ever there were a time for forgiveness, Christmas is it, right?

King Street—the main stretch of shops in charming Old Town Alexandria—was jam-packed with people picking up last-minute gifts, the air filled with that manic energy people have during the holidays. Outside the window of ESP, groups of Prep kids walked back and forth on the sidewalk. Rad and Nikki actually came in for a coffee of their own, but we avoided eye contact and pretended to not see each other—our miserable standard operating procedure at the time.

Palmer was late. Five, ten, and then twenty minutes late.

Finally, he walked in at 2:25 with an apologetic, slightly shell-shocked look. He put his coat on the chair and offered to get me another mocha cappuccino. I started to chatter away, about what, I can't really remember. Palmer warmed his hands on his coffee mug, the color returning to his face after he'd come in from the arctic cold.

But finally he looked up from his black coffee and into

my eyes. Then said—blurted out, really—"Anna, I'm sorry it's been so hard. I couldn't send you a text. I couldn't wait to tell you that—" He paused, and for a heart-stopping second, I thought he was going to finish the sentence with *I love you*.

Instead what I heard was: *We can't hang out anymore.*

Time stopped and then restarted, but it was like I was under water, where everything is very slow and almost silent.

I tried to blink. I couldn't even blink. "I don't . . ." I mumbled. "But *why*?"

"I need to focus on basketball," he said. The sound of his words stretched out like a record on half speed. Palmer looked back into his coffee and then up at me, trying to make a reasonable and apologetic face. "I need to focus on my recovery and next year, and besides, you deserve better, Anna."

So why is it that, despite the fact that Palmer has spent the past month and a half treating me like a stranger, and despite the fact that he dumped me right before Christmas, and even despite the fact that I saw him cozying up to Vanessa just two nights ago, I'm nervous for him tonight? It's because I know how anxious he is. I know that somewhere this afternoon, he was clutching a toilet bowl, sweating. That he might even have had half a beer before he went to the locker room to try to calm himself down. That even with *me* here, my head still swirling with both him and Jethro, no one in this gym is feeling more anxious right now than Palmer.

I hear a whistle signaling that the game's about to begin. I point my Nikon lens at the gym floor, where the proud members of the Prep spirit squad stand flashing their pom-poms. Vanessa's pretty, blond teen-queen pony-tail is bouncing bossily as she barks orders at her less pretty, less blond minions. She says something to Jocelyn, and, though I can't hear what it is, I'm guessing it's a request that Jocelyn tie her shoe, because a second later Jocelyn is on bended knee, fiddling with the laces of Vanessa's size 7 all-white cheerleading sneakers.

Yikes, Jocelyn, get a grip. I snap a picture.

My camera's eye drifts in Palmer's direction. I feel safe behind the Nikon. Palmer's teammates are still in their jackets and sweats, but he's already stripped down to his shorts and tank top, a light sheen of perspiration coating his skin. He's on the free-throw line, a brace—dark blue, to match Prep's navy-and-white colors—on his knee. He sinks the first shot, but the second hits the backboard and bounces off the rim.

I snap a picture as Wallace pats him on the shoulder.

Middle-aged refs in zebra-striped shirts gather at center court. Palmer moves to the middle and stands in a semicrouch directly across from a player from the opposing team, the St. Andrew's Bobcats, his knees bending and unbending, his fingers flexing and unflexing. The whistle blows again, and seconds later Palmer has the ball.

Over the next ten minutes, he takes shot after shot, and I take shot after shot of him in action. He's fast, like the Road Runner, and he hasn't lost an inch off his vertical. True, he makes fewer assists than normal, ignoring wide-open teammates to charge hard to the basket. At one point Wallace mouths, *Dude, what the fu*—? after Palmer hits a low-percentage three-point shot, even though Wallace was jumping up and down, arms waving around like, *Hey, I'm in the paint!*

Whatever watching Palmer is making me feel, I don't think it's love. Maybe it never really was love. The breakup does still feel raw, of course. But the truth is, there are bigger things on my mind. Let's start with how unsure I am about getting into a relationship with Jethro now when I was just in a relationship that swallowed me whole. Or the fact that Jethro talking about next year made all my anxieties about getting into college that much worse. Most of all, the fact that Jethro really, *really* deserves someone who knows what she wants, who doesn't just sleep with him without thinking even a little bit about *his* feelings.

Just before the quarter buzzer, Palmer hits a three-pointer for eighteen points total, setting an all-time personal record, not to mention an all-time school record. As he trots over to the bench, running a gauntlet of high-fives and butt slaps, he looks up unexpectedly, and our eyes lock from fifty feet away.

Apparently he wasn't expecting to see me.

Suddenly I feel like a stalker.

I have as much right to be here as anybody, I tell myself, straightening my spine, tightening my jaw. I have a *duty.* And there's no letting Rad down twice.

But from the hitch in Palmer's step as he walks back onto the court, I can tell: I've broken his concentration.

The second quarter starts, and suddenly Palmer is bricking shots left and right. Which doesn't keep him from taking them. Prep's lead is only nine points now. When Palmer's fourth shot in a row bounces weakly off the rim and the St. Andrew's point guard rips the ball out of the air and sprints down the court for an easy layup, whatever pleasure I might have experienced at seeing I still had the power to distract Palmer turns to dust. I feel sorry for him.

Finally, Prep's coach calls a time-out.

As Palmer and the other players walk to the bench with their heads down, I hear Bill Meade, Palmer's father, yelling above the noise of the crowd. I turn my lens and zoom in for a closer look. Mr. Meade is standing courtside with a wild look in his eyes, smacking his hands together so hard, it must hurt. I'm glad that the camera blocks most of my face as I linger on him and his wife, Palmer's mom, Michelle, who is seated to his left. Palmer's friends call her a MILF right to Palmer's face, and it's such an obvious, incontestable fact that Palmer doesn't even get offended, just laughs and shakes his head, asks only that they use MILMLT (Mother I'd Like to Make Love To).

Mr. Meade is an agribusiness executive (in other words, the boss of a giant corn farm), and Mrs. Meade is a homemaker. They both grew up in Indiana, where Mr. Meade played college basketball. They told me all this when I was at their house for a family dinner just a couple of months ago. They were both pretty friendly and welcoming, despite the fact that I wasn't the kind of girl they were used to seeing Palmer with. So it was a shock when I got a glimpse of the scary intensity hidden beneath Mr. Meade's polite midwestern exterior. When I went to the bathroom, I overheard Mr. Meade through the heating vents, in the next room railing on Palmer about the upcoming season, insisting that he had to prove himself if he was going to reach the highest level. That he had to *focus*. It was a pretty crappy way to talk to a kid with anxiety.

As I stare at Mr. Meade, I wonder—is this the *pressure from all sides* Wallace was talking about back at Vanessa's? Did his parents finally push him too far after the injury, make him think he couldn't handle a girlfriend too?

The ref's whistle blast brings the players back onto the court. Palmer stands at the top of the key, knees bent, fingers fluttering like he's playing an invisible piano. Moments before Dylan Johnson inbounds the ball, Palmer looks up and over. At first I think he's trying to find Prep's coach. But his gaze sweeps right past and gets to the press box and homes right in on me again.

I give him a stupid wave.

The rest of Palmer's second quarter is stellar. Maybe it was my wave, I don't know. Maybe he was feeling guilty and my wave helped him *focus*. Whatever the reason, there are no more lapses in concentration, no more dips in intensity. But St. Andrew's keeps it tight, neither side ever having more than a four-point lead.

In the last five seconds of the half, Dylan inbounds to Wallace, who throws a long pass to Palmer, and Palmer, at least twenty-five feet out from the basket, jumps high in the air, the ball leaving his hands only just before the buzzer goes off.

The ball swishes through the net, not even touching the rim.

The gym explodes, everyone jumping to their feet.

The Prep players circle around Palmer, give him low fives.

Then, a second or two later—before the players can leave the court for halftime, before fans can head to the bathrooms and food trucks outside—the entire gym stops in its tracks. Kanye West's "Good Life" has started blaring over the sound system.

And something's flashing across the giant LCD screen. A headline in big, bold letters:

PRICELESS AT PREP

Suddenly a slide show like the kind people make for birthday parties or weddings begins. Wallace Reid seems to be the star. In a selfie, he shows off that ridiculous, blinding gold chain he wears around his neck. In the next shot, he's got Vanessa and Jocelyn on either arm, but it's really about the bling: he's awkwardly turned sideways, showing off his True Religion jeans and his Yeezy 750 Boosts.

People in the stands start laughing. Cheering. What is this?

Speaking of Yeezy, whoever made this slideshow is doing a damn good job syncing the images with Kanye's lyrics about *a living spree* and how the best things in life aren't free at all.

Did Wallace do this himself?

He's staring up at the LCD, confused. Now he looks to some of his teammates. More looks toward the tech guys in the sound-and-light booth.

Now on the LCD: a Snapchat video that Wallace appears to have shot with a selfie stick while driving around the Prep parking lot in his Mercedes-Benz CLA250 coupe—custom matte-black paint job—the day before school, freestyling: "The Bulldogs are the baddest of the mad, the maddest of the bad, we dominate, berate, captivate, elevate," and, "I'm livin' large, the ladies know I'm in charge," and so on.

From the blank, gaping looks around the court, it's clear nobody knows what the hell this is or why it's playing now.

"You make a PSA for yourself, Wallace?" Dylan shouts out.

Wallace shrugs, but he's enjoying himself—smiling, owning the fact that all eyes are on him. Always quick to follow a trend, Vanessa snaps a couple of cheerleaders into gear, getting them singing and dancing along. A couple of Instas in the stands follow suit.

Not surprisingly, the St. Andrew's players and fans are less enthusiastic. Heads shake and eyes roll. Cries to turn it off come from their side.

The sequence ends with a Vine of Wallace putting on an Alexander McQueen leather-and-python jacket in Neiman Marcus. The Vine loops over and over again, Wallace smirking as his shoulders bulge under the tight leather. Now another headline pops up on the screen in big, bold letters:

ANNUAL SCHOLARSHIP TO PREP FOR
"UNDERPRIVILEGED" ATHLETE: $45K

Wallace definitely did not do this. Someone's mocking the fact that Wallace is technically on financial aid but clearly doesn't need it.

Someone is fighting dirty.

Up comes a new *screenshot* now. It takes me a second, but soon I understand it's a blown-up series of text messages from the phones of various boys on the basketball team. They detail a plan to haze the JV players, make them run a mile around the track at midnight next Wednesday, naked, the slowest guy having to do shots of barbecue sauce.

The look on Wallace's face as he turns to look at Palmer says it all: *Wtf?* But soon it's clear this show isn't over, and what comes next is a shocker: a series of text messages between Wallace and Ms. Sozio, Prep's dance teacher, including such poetic verse as, *Okay, schoolboy, you ready to start learning?* And, *I don't have an apple for you, teacher. But you like bananas better anyway, don't you?*

Now it's clear to everyone what's happening.

Wallace's cell phone has been hacked. In a big way.

Another headline appears:

MULTIPLE HOTEL RENDEZVOUS WITH
A PREP TEACHER: $1K

Oh, wait. Is this like those MasterCard commercials?

Jaws around the gym drop in my peripheral vision. There's a collective *holy shit* in the crowd. My own face is burning red. And none of this has anything to do with me.

Wallace shakes his head, trying to deny it. But Kanye continues:

Welcome to the good life.

And up comes another screenshot: Wallace's dad

forwarded him an email from Mrs. O'Brien, of Prep's financial aid office, which confirms that Wallace has received another year of a *full scholarship* to Prep. On a financial *hardship* basis.

Then the last headline:

GETTING PAID TO PLAY FOR PREP
WHILE LIVING LARGE AND FUCKING
A TEACHER:

PRICELESS

Suddenly the screen goes blank.

Ms. Sozio, who until now has been invisible in the stands, becomes the center of attention as more and more people stare at her. People call her name, and those around her start to step away. She tries to stand strong, ballerina posture in full effect, but it's no match for all the judging eyes, and she quickly slumps.

A Prep mother shouts, "Shame on you!" and one of the gym teachers shuttles Ms. Sozio out of the gym.

Now all eyes are back on Wallace. "What? I'm *eighteen!*" he calls out. But a few of his Prep teammates, evidently shocked, start to put more space between them and him. People in the stands are starting to shout stuff at him, some congratulatory, some ugly.

Wallace breathes heavily, shoulders rising and falling. Anger, shame, and fear swirl on his face. Palmer is talking to him, trying to calm him down, but, like a wild animal cornered, Wallace reacts instinctively. Suddenly he's tearing through the stands, leaping over benches, not caring if he knocks into people or steps on them.

Soon everyone realizes who he's after: Haven.

I point my camera to get a better look. Rad's already staring at me, wide-eyed, desperately trying to communicate something. I finally get it—her lips and arm motions are saying: *You better be catching this!*

I start clicking away.

Haven's laughing louder than anybody, literally shaking with laughter.

Of course: *this* is Haven's style.

When Wallace reaches him, he cocks back his fist. Haven doesn't flinch or put up his hands to defend himself. He just keeps laughing, evidently too stoned to be concerned. It will be tough to sustain that laugh while spitting out broken teeth.

Andrew launches himself in front of Haven just in time, and the three guys tumble and roll into the aisle, Haven and Andrew coming out on top, Haven sitting on Wallace's chest, Andrew pinning Wallace's arms. The crowd really starts to go nuts, seeing Wallace brought down by a techie and a stoner-jock. Palmer leaps up into the stands and tries to break it up. To pull Wallace back down onto the court.

But suddenly everyone freezes as a mechanical voice roars throughout the gym: *"If you want to see all of Wallace Reid and more, visit Prepfortruth.com."*

9

"It's so crazy," I say, lying on Rad's bed an hour later. "His whole life is just out here for everyone to see."

"Don't waste your sympathy," Rad says, handing me a cup of freshly brewed tea. "He probably uses the same password for everything, and that password is probably one-two-three-four or his birthday or the name of his pet gerbil or something."

"You think?" I say uncertainly, then: "Mmm, this tea rules."

"Dad makes killer chai. Anyway, Wallace will come out of this fine. I'm sure his buds are just bursting with pride that he was sleeping with hot little Ms. Sozio."

For the rest of the night, we'll be doing what every other kid at Prep is doing: violating Wallace's privacy. I never realized what a great distraction from my own problems violating *someone else's* privacy could be. It's pretty twisted, actually. But it gets worse too: I'd love to tell you that I cared about the inner workings of Wallace Reid. But the honest, ugly truth is, Wallace isn't who I want to know more about.

I need to know WTF Wallace was talking about the other night when he said those things about Palmer. I'm hoping the answers lie somewhere on Prepfortruth.com.

I can't shake his mysterious words. Wallace called me cool. *Too cool.* He even brushed off Vanessa. I may have been a sheet or two to the wind at that point, but no amount of beer could make that conversation seem normal. As grateful as I am to be on the road to recovery with my friends, back where I belong, there's this annoying itch at the back of my brain that I need to scratch like a mother. I need some kind of closure.

Rad has already changed into her ancient *Hannah Montana* crop top and her flannel PJ bottoms and popped in her Invisalign retainer. Suddenly she starts laughing so hard, it sounds like she's wheezing.

"What?"

"Wallace must take two dozen shirtless selfies a day. And he sends the same ones to Jocelyn as he does to Ms. Suzio. He doesn't even customize." Rad makes a *tsk-tsk* sound. "Wallace, you're not just cheesy, you're lazy too. Bad combo." She swivels the screen around to show me a shot of Wallace flexing in front of a mirror, sucking in his cheeks to accentuate his jawline and pouting Kylie Jenner–style. She swivels the screen back. "And whenever he goes to the mall, he sends his mother pictures of his clothes from the dressing room. *That's* who he was sending that ridiculous snap of himself trying on that python-leather jacket to?"

"We do that too, Rad," I point out.

"We're not dudes."

"How long do you think it's going to take for Wallace's parents' lawyers to get this thing taken down?"

Rad's eyes scan the screen. "Who knows? This is freaking *endless*. So much to parse. His entire iPhone must've just gotten dumped. There's stuff going back almost a year. Do you think we can print any of it in the *Xandria*?"

"Probably not."

Her face, glowing from the unhealthy distance it is from the screen, falls a little. I nuzzle up to her to see the screen. Whether she can print it or not, the amount of Wallace's stuff that's been dumped here is overwhelming. My eyes start randomly picking out lines in which I recognize other names, mostly Instagrams.

A text exchange between Wallace and Jack Connolly, another senior:

Wallace: Who's hotter Kate Upton or Hannah Davis?
Jack: Upton.
Wallace: Right answer.

Or this, with Meg Clare, a senior, midpyramid spirit squadder:

Wallace: Joss told me you have the geo tests from last year?
Meg: Sorry, threw 'em out

Wallace: Damn!
Wallace: What r u doing tonight? Come help me study.

Palmer's name jumps out at me everywhere, of course. I'm trying to play it cool right now with Rad—to not even let her sense what my real curiosity is about. But I can't keep my eyes from focusing anywhere else.

From a few weekends ago:

Palmer: Yo Wally come play Madden. My mom's gonna order pizza.
Wallace: Yo I'll CUM over if I can be your moms pizza boy. Tell her I deliver!
Palmer: Don't, dude. Seriously.

From the beginning of the basketball season:

Wallace: That game was ratchet! Get these underclass hos to the gym pronto.

I notice, relieved, that Palmer never replied to this.

"Amazing how little guys talk when they talk," Rad says, shaking her head.

"You're so right . . . ," I agree. "Almost nothing about how anyone *feels*."

"Oh my God!" Rad exclaims. "Except for these." She points to the screen.

Wallace: Dude Jocelyn takes so long to finish I don't think I'll ever get this crick out of my neck! I've gotta

stay away from her before game nights! Jump shot's
gonna be off!

And:

Wallace: Ms S likes me to wear her undies when I'm in
her class. #pussywhipped.

We spiral into a giggle fit, Rad bent into the fetal position, clutching her stomach.

"This is the most I've worked out in years!" she hoots.

I wipe at the tears streaming from my eyes. When I sober up from wheeze-laughing, I say, "Can we look for stuff
about Palmer? About Palmer and me."

"That's clearly an awful, self-destructive idea . . . but
fine." Rad rips the laptop away and types my name into the
search box. Then she starts summarizing Palmer's texts in
which my name comes up:

"You and Palmer are going to a movie, so you can't hang
out with Wallace. Neither you nor Jocelyn has seen any of
the *Mission: Impossible* movies, and Wallace just can't believe how chicks have no appreciation for fine action cin-
ema. Blah, blah, blah. How did you choose these snoozefest
losers over *moi*, Anna? I'll never understand. . . ."

Rad scrolls faster. "Okay, what's Palmer's cell number?
Let's just search it and put you out of your misery."

I give it to her. Rad's fingers fly across the keyboard.
"Bingo!"

A messenger thread from late September:

Wallace: Hey man, sick moves at practice today. You gotta help me with my fade this weekend. Still down to shoot? We can roll to Vanessa's together after. Dude, that girl wants you bad. No foreplay necessary, if you know what I mean . . .

Palmer: Hey. Definitely down to ball. You can come to my place, we got a half court out back. Gonna pass on the party, though. Anna and I are seeing a movie. . . . A little foreplay necessary ;)

Wallace: Anna? That weirdo art girl?? Does she even know how to talk? Not that talking matters. Dude, Vanessa's a SURE THING. #Readyandwaiting.

Now Rad finds a text exchange from right after Christmas:

Palmer: You around? I'm bored af.

Wallace: Thought you'd be with Anna. She away?

Palmer: Nah.. Just getting tired of that.

Wallace: Aww yeaahh wore out that pony?

Palmer: lol u could say that

Palmer: Don't wanna worry about it anymore

Rad tenses next to me as we finish reading it aloud. "Wow," she says. "What an asshole. You okay?"

I nod, breathing deeply through my nose. Maybe that's all I was to him. A weird girl he thought he could get with, but couldn't, so he moved on. Maybe this is the closure I was looking for. I just wish it felt a little better.

"Guys are dicks—" But now Rad stops short.

"What?"

"Anna . . ."

"What?"

"You see this?" Rad asks. Her tone is serious, the same one she uses for newspaper meetings and when talking to her father. It snaps me from anxious to attentive. I lean in close to the screen with her, almost cheek to cheek. "Whoa."

She points me to a group text from November that hopped between Wallace, Palmer, and Dylan Johnson.

Wallace: Got Juice brahh?

Palmer: Man, I'm struggling hard.

Dylan: Your knee bothering you still?

Palmer: Kind of . . . idk it's weird. I just don't feel 💯

Wallace: You need some of D's holy water

Palmer: ?

Dylan: ha I like that

Wallace: lol that beyonce song would be your theme

Wallace: 🎵 I NEED YOUR HALO HALO HALOOOO

Palmer: seriously ?????

Dylan: If you need a boost I can help u out. 💪

Palmer: Ohh okay. I'll call you later

Rad already has another tab open, diligently researching, while my stomach has wound itself into the tightest of knots. But I already know what they're saying.

Know that sinking feeling that comes right before someone tells you something awful, that split second when you

104

see the look in their eyes and your stomach turns to pins and needles? Could this be what Wallace was talking about?

Are they taking steroids?

We non-Instas may joke about the reigning clique, suggesting their teenage superstardom doesn't come naturally—and don't get me wrong, there are plenty of sweet-sixteen boob jobs and bottle blondes to provide the seeds for those rumors—but to have actual evidence, black-and-white text damning three of our starting basketball players as cheaters . . . well, that sinking feeling pretty much sums it up.

"This is huge," Rad says. "Like, Lance Armstrong huge."

Now she's clicking and typing like mad, in full journalist mode. *Halo* is another slangish term for a certain steroid, Rad relays, and seconds later she's on a page outlining the NCAA bylaws. I close my eyes, breathe.

"Does it say they actually *took* them anywhere?" I ask finally.

Rad pauses, biting her lip, then sighs. "Well . . . no. Wallace might be dumb as rocks, but Palmer was smart enough to do business over the phone or in person."

"If he even did—"

"Seriously, Anna? You're gonna defend him right now?"

Her words are sharp, but I push past them. "We can't know for sure. You just said there isn't evidence—"

"This isn't an episode of *Suits*. What more do you need?"

"Even if this isn't true, Palmer could lose scholarships, not get into college, ruin his life over nothing. Nobody deserves that," I say, surprised by my own persistence.

Rad leans back. "Like how you threw away *your* social life? Over a dumb jock?"

I think she might start shouting, but she can see I'm upset, and suddenly now, she softens. "Palmer got in your head last semester, but this has to be obvious to you now. He's a dick. Don't give him the benefit of anything."

I love her for feeling protective of me, even after I've been such a bad friend. Yet, against all the good judgment in the world, I want to text Palmer. Part of me *is* trying to give him the benefit of the doubt. Innocent until proven guilty, right? Maybe part of me can't believe I threw my friends away for someone who was lying to me the whole time and who told his friend he was tired of me. Last but not least: did I screw everything up with Jethro by letting him believe I *might* still like this guy?

Rad yawns and (as if reading my manic thoughts) adds, "If you hadn't pulled a *Gone Girl* on your real friends, we would've been there to point out the warning signs. Maybe even saved Christmas, Cindy Lou Who–style."

Slipping under the covers, I tell her I've got a headache from staring at the screen for so long. "Okay, okay. Enough for now."

She snaps out the light and gets under the covers with me.

"Hey, Rad?" I say into the dark.

"Yeah?"

"You know I love you, right?"

Silence. "Show, don't tell," she says.

At least I'm not alone right now.

10

Monday morning.

Thirty-six hours since Wallace's phone was hacked. Going on seventy-two since I've seen or heard from Jethro.

By last night, the court of Prep opinion had already ruled that Palmer, Dylan, and Wallace must be *juicing*. Some people think the basketball season should be canceled entirely. Some think the guys should be suspended. No one cares that there isn't any proof. Or that they're all denying it completely. Saying it was a joke.

Then there's Haven. In Twitter debates, pro-Haven factions use the hashtag *#Havenis4real*. Late last night, a few members of the basketball team who got smeared in the leak started the *#Haveninhell* hashtag. It was accompanied by a Photoshopped pic of Haven's head on a spit.

I'm wasting time thinking about boys and jocks, though. The art show's less than ten days away, so I slip into the lab early, around seven a.m. Mr. Touhey leaves the art studio unlocked so we can hang out and work before or after school. I'm relieved as the knob gives way easily and I pass into my sanctuary without having to talk to anyone.

But as I'm taking my painting out of its cubby, a voice behind me says, "Hey."

I jump, my nerves lighting up, and spin around, nearly dropping my armful of paints. One of the tubes slips from the crook of my elbow, plopping onto the tile.

"Hi," I say, dumping the rest of the paint onto the table.

Jethro steps forward and picks up the tube.

How is he *always* popping up when I least expect it?

He's just a lurker, like I am, on social media, so I couldn't even stalk him this weekend. After a moment of painful silence, we both start talking at the same time.

"Sorry," I say with an uneasy laugh. "You first."

"I saw what Palmer wrote," he says finally.

"Oh," I say, surprised. I didn't think Jethro had a cruel bone in his body. It's not like him to kick a girl while she's down (or kick a girl at all, really), but I guess I deserve this after all I've put him through.

"Yeah," I say. "Kinda crazy."

"I mean about *you*," he says now. "I'm sorry. You holding up okay?"

There's the boy I know. "Others got it a lot worse," I say.

Jethro nods. "No question. But I'm sure it was hard for you. Especially given . . . the way you might still feel about him."

I look down at the ground. *It's so much more complicated than that,* I want to say. But all I muster is a lame, "Oh. Okay. Thanks."

Now he says, "Look, about that. I'm really sorry about how I reacted on Friday. It was really immature, and I shouldn't have stormed off. It's just . . . it was hard to hear."

Unspoken words hang in the air, floating around in the sharp chemical smells of glue and glaze and paint thinner. I don't know what to say, too afraid it'll be the wrong thing. I focus on fighting the overwhelming urge to reach for him.

"Have you talked to him?" he asks finally.

"Palmer?"

"Yeah."

I shake my head.

"Andrew heard he's gonna be out today," Jethro says, "maybe all week. His parents are, like, freaking out, I guess. Talking to coaches and stuff."

The last thing I want to talk about with Jethro right now is Palmer. So I use an age-old SAD coping mechanism— changing the subject.

"Speaking of skipping school, you think we'll see Prep's very own Edward Snowden around today?"

"Haven?"

"Who else?"

A beat passes, and then Jethro says, "We don't know he did this."

I snort. "You don't think he did?"

"He hasn't told me or Andrew anything."

"How come?"

"We couldn't reach him all weekend. He hasn't returned any of our texts."

"Wait. So he's, like . . . in hiding or something?"

Jethro looks contemplative. "I don't know. I mean, I guess he has been going, like, toe to toe with Wallace this year."

"Really?" (Something I'd know if I'd been around, I guess.)

Jethro nods. "Right before break, Haven and Andrew were out back smoking, and Wallace drove by with Vanessa and threw a Big Gulp at them. It didn't hit them, but it nailed Haven's bag, fried his laptop. I haven't seen him that mad, like, ever."

I sigh. "Well, why didn't he tell anyone?"

"And tell Nichols he and Andrew were blazing before class?"

"Oh, right. That sucks."

Jethro smiles, a thought creeping across his face. "Know where I'd rather be?"

I shrug. "Tell me."

"The Stairway to Heaven. Oahu Island, Hawaii. They call them the Haiku Stairs, and they're not even open to the public. But we could pack some beers and find our way to the top of the cliff. Views a thousand feet down the mountain."

"Maybe without the beers," I say. "Had enough of those for a while."

He nods. After a long pause he says, "I hope you know,

if you ever need someone to talk to, I'm . . . here. Whatever happened, I'm your friend. I'll always be your friend."

"Thank you. It means a lot."

Jethro hands me the paint tube, which I take with a clammy hand, then turns to go. What I ever did to deserve his friendship, let alone anything more, is beyond me.

When he's gone, I pull my phone from the bottom of my bag.

I can't take it any longer. I send a single line of text.

Are you okay?

I wait a full minute. Palmer doesn't respond.

For the entire day I avoid eye contact, pretend not to hear my name being spoken, and try to blend into my surroundings like those twig bugs you see on the Discovery Channel. An announcement during lunch told us that last period is canceled today for an emergency assembly. I'm headed to swap books so I can make a quick getaway right after, and I find Nikki waiting for me at my locker.

"Hey," she says, her voice gentle. "How are you?"

I force a smile. It's weirdly worrying when other people worry about me. Makes me feel guilty. There's just no winning with anxiety. "I'm okay. How are you?"

"Eh. Mattie texted me once last night."

"That's good, right?"

"He just seems so . . . noncommittal. Like, I can't even

get him to commit to texting me back more than once a day. Much less to when we're gonna hang out."

"Like every boy ever."

"Haven's gonna be in such deep shit with the whole Wallace thing," Nikki says, changing the subject.

"Do you think he could lose his place at MIT?"

Nikki's eyes go wide. "Hadn't thought of that. Is there even any, like, hard evidence? Can they trace back through all that techie stuff like on *CSI*?"

"I have no idea."

"I talked to him yesterday. He wanted me to pick up his chem assignments."

"You talked to him? Did he do this?"

"Yeah," she says. "He thinks Wallace deserved it." She pauses meaningfully. "But he also told me to tell you that you didn't deserve to get dragged into it."

Nikki promised to sit with some of her Thesbo friends, so I slide into a middle pew in the chapel beside Rad. Jethro and Andrew sit behind us. I tap my toe nervously. Andrew won't care about what happened with me and Jethro. But every time I'm with Jethro and Rad together now, some part of me is preparing for Rad's wrath when she finds out. It won't even matter that Jethro's (seemingly) okay now.

You've messed up enough of us for one year, she said.

Headmaster Nichols takes the pulpit. Before he speaks, though, a male voice yells out, "You tapped that ass, son!"

Wallace sits in the front row, where no Instagram has

ever sat before. He doesn't turn or move, but you can almost feel him wanting to raise his fist in triumph.

Scattered shouts of "Yeah, boy!" and "Work it, Wallace!"

"Pig!" responds a girl.

More laughter all around us.

Rad lets out a low whistle. "Wow," she says. "Get ready for a battle of the sexes."

"Quiet! Quiet! And phones away!" Headmaster Nichols says. "Anyone who does not comply with this order will have their phone confiscated."

Teachers and admin are wound tight today.

Nichols glowers as kids pocket their cells. "All of you are aware of the troubling events that occurred at the basketball game on Saturday evening," he continues. "A student's private information was made public. That student is senior Wallace Reid, and there are some allegations that are being investigated currently."

I assume he'll bring up the steroids. But he doesn't.

"To that end," he says, "Ms. Sozio has elected to go on administrative leave for the rest of the semester. The senior administrative council has issued a formal investigation into Ms. Sozio's conduct. We here at Prep take transgressions of student–teacher boundaries very seriously."

Behind us I hear Andrew lean over to Jethro. "Notice he's not talking about canceling a state-championship basketball season."

I have to keep my eyes fixed on Nichols to stop myself from turning around to see the look on Jethro's face.

"There have been other accusations," Nichols continues. "But Mr. Reid has acted honorably over the last forty-eight hours and has voiced his intention to accept the punishment his parents and the honor board see fit to dole out. Mostly, however, we need to remember that the students affected by this violation are *victims*. Mr. Reid's privacy has been terribly invaded. In a way no one deserves."

Rad snorts and whispers, "Oh my God. Yeah, let's all weep for Wall—"

Suddenly the sound of buzzing sweeps over the chapel. Teachers can't hear one vibration. Two hundred is a different story.

"It's like a sex toy convention," Rad says, and we crack up.

Most people are digging in their pockets or bags for their phones.

Nichols is repeating his threats again. *Do not take out your phones. Detention. No extracurriculars.*

No one seems to care. Strength in numbers and all that.

"No . . . way," Rad says, opening a browser window.

I glance down. Prepfortruth.com is on her screen.

"Wallace isn't the only 'victim' now," she says.

11

"HOLE E. SHIT!" A DETACHED VOICE NOT FAR FROM ME SAYS.

Know what murmuring sounds like between points at a tennis match? That's an adult murmur. What's growing inside the chapel right now sounds nothing like that. It sounds more like a crowd waiting for Beyoncé at RFK Stadium.

Wallace's deepest, darkest secrets arrived with a bang—images and text splashed up on a huge LCD. Spectacle, just as Haven and God intended it. Today's hack, however, has spread with a *hmmm, hmmm, hmmm*—as a quiet, almost beautiful symphony of softly vibrating phones swelling throughout the chapel.

"*Off*," Nichols says from the podium. "Not on vibrate or silent or in airplane mode. Off. Now. Then put *yourselves* on silent mode, please."

Some goody kids start powering down their phones.

Mine's still buried in my bag, where I try to always keep it. Rad's less inclined to follow Nichols's order; her phone sits low on her high-waisted jeans, and she's scanning the alerts.

When I whirl around, I see Jethro's doing the same, his face a mix of confusion and disbelief. People are all whispering: *Prep for Alexis Bowman.*

I glance over in the general direction of the Instagrams. I can't see Alexis anywhere, but I do see Wallace. He's openly and flagrantly staring at his phone, doesn't give a crap about Nichols. A toothy smile is creeping across his face.

Rad's on the home screen of Prepfortruth.com, whispering the details.

Alexis Bowman. Second-tier Insta. Alternate on the spirit squad. Alexis's secret biggie: kleptomania. Not shoplifting. Actual kleptomania. In her Gmail account was a letter officially banning her from Tysons Galleria.

"It's everything," Rad whispers in my ear, too excitedly. "All her stuff, like with Wallace. The shoplifting's just clickbait to get people digging for more."

Up front, Ms. Dominick, Prep's most senior, severe Latin teacher, is whispering in Headmaster Nichols's ear. He leans into the mic. "Everyone stay here until you're excused by Ms. Dominick. Anyone who leaves or continues to use his or her phone will be subject to disciplinary measures. I'm very serious about this." Nichols then hurries off.

"I thought Haven kinda liked Alexis," I whisper back to the boys behind us. "He said she was hot."

Rad interjects before either of them can. "Hell hath no fury like a troll scorned. Do you see her anywhere?"

I scan the room again and finally spot Alexis. She's sitting toward the middle with a few other Instas. Alexis is one of those almost strawberry-blond redheads with impossibly perfect color and freckles in just the right places. She doesn't look angry or even embarrassed.

Just . . . stunned into silence.

Wallace is beaming. He knows he's about to be yesterday's news. Kleptomania is one thing. But what's on everyone's mind—the reason everyone is dying to get to a private place where phones are allowed—is what *else* is buried in Alexis's files. Wallace had some blood the vampires could feed on, including the stuff about Palmer. But Alexis is an Instagram *girl*, and that means she can be counted on to have gossiped about and insulted half the *other* girls in school, including the rest of her Insta clique.

The buzz begins again.

Phones vibrating. More alerts.

There's *more* coming.

Dylan Johnson.

Instagram of the first order. Power forward on the basketball team, kind-of-friend of Palmer, third man in the already infamous juice/holy water exchange that's got Palmer MIA today. But this time Dylan's clickbait has nothing to do with steroids. Now we're looking at a text from months ago to his ex-girlfriend, none other than *Vanessa.*

Dylan: Yeah, it hurts. But that Valtrex stuff helps. But also, maybe I got it from you. Ever think of that?

Vanessa: You're telling me you might have given me fucking herpes and are trying to blame me?

My eyes make a beeline for Vanessa. She's sitting with her spirit-squad friends, her head a little bit higher than the others, and her minions clearly have no idea how to deal with their captain and queen bee in this situation. Vanessa smiles tightly at the people around her, then picks up her phone and starts texting someone, as if nothing's happened. As if she's making plans to meet someone at the Fashion Centre at Pentagon City later.

Dylan, though, is now glaring in our direction. He's surprisingly short for a basketball player, but, herpes or not, he is definitely cute. Brown eyes and Bieber hair. Wholesome-looking but apparently not that wholesome-acting. Not to judge—I'm sure some fantastic people have herpes.

Dylan stands and points at Jethro and Andrew. "Tell your dickwad friend to watch his back."

Ms. Dominick walks down the aisle. "Sit down, Mr. Johnson."

For some reason, her saying his last name out loud elicits a cackle from one corner of the room, plus a stray boy's voice: "Oooh, *burn*, Mr. Johnson."

Before the boys can respond to Dylan, it happens. Again.

This time it's *Josh Klein*—backup shortstop for the Prep baseball team. Haven has outed him for having cheated on three AP exams last year alone. A fact he *admitted* in a snap to his swimmer girlfriend! Adios, Cornell, I guess.

On the right-hand side of the aisle, Josh just shrugs to his friends. Clearly trying to play it off, no big thang. But I can see it already—the glimmer of fear in his eyes.

Alexis, Dylan, Josh, and a little Vanessa Eubanks for collateral damage? Even with the Palmer situation as it is, even though I'd die a slow death if someone did this to *me*—this is . . . kinda twistedly awesome. And with Haven at the wheel, I have to admit I feel safe; he won't do this to any of *us*. Sure, these are real people with real feelings. But how can you not feel a little schadenfreude when cheats, kleptos, and a basketball player who doesn't give a shit about anyone but himself catch a little bit of Haven's technoshrapnel?

"Dude," Andrew whispers, leaning forward on my other side now. "Haven musta found a way into *all* their phones."

Before I can respond, more whispers fill the hall. All eyes turn toward the prettiest girl in the sophomore class. Beneath heavy mascara and probably a year's worth of Latisse on her lashes, I see her eyes go dark.

Number five is live.

It's *Colleen Wahtera*. The most judgmental girl in school. Nightmare by any standards. Not even an official Instagram yet because she's only a sophomore. But she *was* a shoo-in until this very minute. Only now, flashing across our screens: a Twitter DM asking her cousin how she can get an abortion and keep it a secret from her cray-cray ultrareligious parents. Brutal.

People don't know what to think about this one. Is it laughing material? I know it isn't for me. Welcome to half the reason sex scares me. Colleen stares forward at Ms.

Dominick, not responding to her friends, who are touching her on her back, giving whatever sympathy mini-Instas are humanly capable of. Colleen won't even look at them.

I turn back to Jethro and Andrew. "That's a horrible thing for Haven to put out there. What's that asshole doing?"

Andrew just shrugs. Jethro looks stunned. Says only one word: "Sucks."

Rad whispers, "True. It sucks. Really sucks. But Colleen? Let's be honest: H couldn't have chosen a bitchier girl. I mean, that time she called Hannah Moyer a whore in front of the whole cafeteria for too much PDA? Karma's a bitch."

Ms. Dominick obviously doesn't know any specifics of what's happening on the ground. But, sensing another leak and unable to chain our hands to our chairs and away from our phones, she immediately leans in to the mic at the podium again. "If you all ever want to leave this room, you better start acting like adults," she continues. "You could be here a while. In fact, if this behavior continues, anyone who was planning to take an early bus home better start thinking about a plan B."

It's the exact wrong moment to accidentally bring up the morning-after pill. My dad once made me listen to an NPR podcast about the definition of *fiasco*. Apparently it's the moment when a crowd loses itself entirely. When every little thing seems like the funniest thing anyone has ever heard, even when it's not funny at all. Like an abortion. Anyway, we're there, apparently. *Fiasco*. Ms. Dominick could tell us her kid was dying of lupus and there had been a *Red Dawn*–like attack by North Korea right outside, and the laughter would only get worse.

Fighting tears, Colleen sinks down. The one last piece of dignity she has left is that she has not yet let the room see her cry. People see the look on her face, and for a moment the room goes silent again.

Ten seconds later, Colleen's luck really changes. So does that of everyone else who's been leaked . . . for the moment.

Number six is a doozy.

The first announcement comes from Wallace's mouth as he shouts across the room at Mattie. "Whaaaaa? You actors are messed up!"

"Oh no," Rad says, opening the link. "This is *no bueno*."

Abortion is the aftermath of sex—or *some* sex, anyway. It has shock value to my classmates, but, let's face it, it's a lot *less* exciting than sex itself. And sex itself is what the sixth leak hands everyone on a platter: a link to everything that's been uploaded to or sent from Mattie Eizenberg's Instagram Direct.

I look over at Mattie, seated on the left side of the aisle. Unlike Dylan and Josh, he's not even pretending to be fine with it. He keeps reaching up to check that absurdly blond man bun, making sure it hasn't fallen off. A couple of his actor friends are whispering in his ear; some are even smiling a little. But Mattie looks white. Like, Kristen Stewart white.

Rad gives me glimpses of the series of pictures as she scans through. The tasteless grape-flavored gum I'm still chewing from after lunch almost falls out of my mouth.

"Oh Jesus," I whisper. "We shouldn't look at these. Gross."

But Rad keeps going. There are almost forty pics. It's a mix of half- and fully naked pics and sexted private-parts selfies. These aren't models or RedTube screenshots. These are girls we *know*. Every one of the pics is full-on amateur and real and obviously taken with a phone. Then passed to one of the boys and finally on to Mattie for him to rank.

In the pics that show faces, there are so many I recognize. Acquaintances. Class friends. Facebook friends. Worst of all, I soon see, faces aren't necessary. Mattie has labeled every one of the nearly forty pics with a hashtag of each girl's name—and either a letter or a number, and a symbol: #HelenMcNultyJ♠, #AmyK9♦, #MeredithAndrews5♥, #DianeJackson8♣.

"It's a deck of cards," Rad says. "He's rating girls according to their value. Spades, diamonds, hearts, clubs."

Even though I've seen only a couple of the photos, I've seen enough to know that this is bad. Really bad. I turn around and see Mattie's looking down at the ground, somber, like he knows that the only thing holding those girls back from ripping the skin right off his body is the threat of suspension.

"I don't know who I hate more right now: Mattie or Haven."

Rad puts her phone down, out of view. Her face falls. "Nikki's on here . . ."

"What . . . ? Did Nik send that loser a picture the night they—?"

Rad shakes her head slowly. "No."

"Then what?"

"She didn't send anything. I think he took it when she was asleep or something. He found the perfect angle to show every inch of her. Worst of all, he gave Nikki the two of clubs. Lowest in the deck."

"I'm gonna rip his tiny balls off . . ." I grit my teeth, scanning the crowd for Nikki.

Rad's gaze drops to the ground, and now, for the first time in years, I see tears start to form in her eyes. "*Oh my God*, Anna."

"What? There's more?"

Rad looks panicked. "I put so much pressure on Nikki to—"

"No," I cut her off, "this is not your fault. This is Mattie Eizenfuck's fault. And the fault of every other sick loser bro who sent him their pictures."

I stand and turn back toward Mattie. My mouth feels dry and my head feels light, but for the first time in days, I don't feel anxious at all. Rage is the ultimate cure for that.

"Anna, don't do it," Andrew says, looking up at me. "I'll beat his ass later."

From behind me I hear Ms. Dominick say, "Ms. Soler, take your seat."

But I don't. I'm going to rip the man bun right off Mattie's head—literally scalp him in front of everyone. I walk to the aisle and head in the direction of Mattie. I feel my hand form a fist, almost involuntarily.

Then it happens.

In the corner of my eye, I see Nikki stand up, phone in hand. She looks like she's in shock, like she's sleepwalking.

She wavers a little, and a couple of people nearby reach out to try to stop her from falling to the ground. But Nikki doesn't fall. She just looks at the chapel door, breaks into a sprint, and slams the door after her.

"Nikki?" I call over the bathroom stall.

"I don't want to talk, Anna."

"Please let me in."

"No."

"Let's leave. We can go to my house. Or anywhere. But you don't want to sit in there, looking at those gross things no one should look at. And I swear, Nikki. We're not going to let him get away with it."

Nikki breathes loudly. "It's not just those pictures. It's every text I sent him for the last month. Haven didn't just hack his Instagram and leak those pics. He put everything of Mattie's out there. Everything he uploaded or wrote online."

I open the next stall and climb up onto the toilet to look down. She's fully clothed, sitting on the pot. But Nikki doesn't glance up or move.

"Why do you care what that asshole said, after what he did?"

Nikki stays silent a long time before finally looking up at me. "You've never been in love, have you, A?"

I think of Jethro. Then step down and wait. I'll stay here as long as I have to.

"I haven't been accepted to any schools yet," Nikki says. "What if I get rejected because of this? This is going to be online forever."

"Schools aren't gonna see this, Nik. And, even if they did, Mattie's the one who won't be getting into any schools."

We sit in silence for a minute. I send Haven a nasty text telling him to *stop doing this shit now*, but he doesn't respond.

Suddenly someone else whips into the bathroom.

I know those footsteps.

Next thing I know, I hear Rad's boot kick in Nikki's bathroom door.

"Come on, sweetie. Let's go home. I'm so sorry I got you into this. I'm so, so sorry. I hate myself," she says.

I squeeze out of my stall, and the three of us melt into a group hug. If Rad weren't so upset, she'd cringe at the corniness.

We drive Nikki home, and Rad spends the whole time saying she's sorry. The only thing Nikki says the whole way home is *You didn't do anything*, and it seems like she means it. She isn't mad at Rad. She's just . . . destroyed. The mocking, vicious things Mattie said about her to his friends might even be worse than the deck of cards.

I hate that little shit like I've never hated anyone.

An hour later Nikki's in her bed. I can hear enough through her whimpers to understand that she wants her mom.

"You sure?" I ask. Nikki nods an affirmative.

Rad calls Nikki's mom at the hairdresser, where she's getting a blowout for some charity event tonight, and explains what's happened. Andrea comes through the door twenty minutes later, says a harried hello, then immediately pours herself a gin and tonic and downs half of it before going up to Nikki's room.

"Want us to stay?" I ask when she returns a couple of minutes later.

"That's very nice, girls," Andrea says with an unusually sympathetic, sincere tone. "But Nik should probably just rest. I canceled my event. I'll be here with her."

12

HAVEN LIVES LESS THAN TWO MILES FROM PREP. SINCE HIS DAD works for the DEA, he travels a lot, so Haven is usually home alone. Haven always says he could stay inside for a year as long as he had his computer and an Internet connection. After the emotional and physical beat-down Rad and I are about to give him, he might be able to test that theory.

"There," Rad says as we turn the corner into Haven's cul-de-sac. She points silently at the house, perched at the end of the circle. Rad's spent most of the past half hour saying one word at a time, grunting, barely making eye contact. She feels guilty about Nikki, but I've gone the other way, ready to scream at Mattie, at Haven, at anyone.

When Rad and I pull into the driveway, we hit something, and it crunches beneath my tires. Shit. I back up, trying to get off whatever the hell it is.

We get out and find that we've knocked two black garbage bags over and they've vomited all over the driveway. Some of it's regular trash (delivery containers left over from the food Haven eats every night), but about half of each thirty-gallon bag is filled with what look like old video game cartridges, all of which seem to be for a game about that *E.T.* movie. (No, I've never seen it—sue me.) "He's such a freak," Rad says.

We ring the bell and knock on the door.

When no one answers, Rad yells Haven's name loudly enough to attract the attention of a couple of neighbors, including an old lady with a Boston terrier who pops her head outside her door, then retreats.

Rad keeps knocking and calling Haven's name. His dad's obviously not here, and if Haven is, he's putting on a good show. There isn't a single light on in the house.

Rad starts walking around the side of the craftsman house. I follow. She reaches her hand behind a wooden gate with peeling white paint, just squeezing her arm inside. She unlatches the clasp and tells me to follow. It's not the first time I've broken into someone's backyard with Rad (usually there's a pool involved), but when she leads me into the carport behind the house and starts searching around, I don't understand.

"What are you looking for?"

Finally Rad marches over to a monstrosity of wires jutting out of a small plastic box attached to the wall of the carport. One by one she starts yanking them out of the socket and letting them drop to the ground.

Nothing happens.

"Now what?" I ask, confused.

Rad looks at her phone. Checking the time. "Wait for it," she says, holding her middle finger in the air like it's a universal sign for waiting, then pointing it in the direction of the back door. "Wait for it . . . five, four, three, two, one, zero, negative one, negative two—"

Only two seconds off the bull's-eye, the door pops open. No lights have been turned on, but there's no question that it's the silhouette of a boy, not Haven's dad.

"What'd you do?" Haven asks.

Rad walks toward him. "Figured you might starve to death before coming out, but two minutes without a Web connection, and voilà. A jerk-off reappears right in front of our eyes. It's like Criss Angel in reverse."

"Rad, if this is about Nikki, I didn't know . . ."

"Of course it's about Nikki. She's supposed to be your friend. You should see her right now. She asked for her *mom.* That's how bad this is."

I think about walking up to him and spitting right in his face, and I barely hold myself back. Picturing Nikki alone in her room, crying, I chime in with the first thing I can think of. "You did that to her *and* you made her get all your stupid chem lab assignments? *Today?* Who does that?"

Haven steps into a small pool of moonlight. His face is paler, and with deeper, darker circles under his eyes, than I've ever seen.

"I didn't do anything to Nikki," he says.

Rad lays into him. "Fine, whatever, you did it to Mattie, which screwed over Nikki. You knew they were together that night. You probably knew what he was up to."

"And you must have looked at what was in there," I say.

"No, I swear, I didn't."

Rad raises her voice for the first time. "I saw your pervy virgin YouPorn browsing history over break, remember? When you hit eighteen it'll basically be a felony. You want us to believe you just leaked a bunch of photos of naked girls and didn't even look at them?"

Haven goes a little red. "I didn't look. And if I did, I would have deleted any picture of Nikki, of course. But—"

"But what?"

"I didn't leak those pics."

"You expect us to believe that after we know you leaked Wallace's stuff?" I ask.

"No. I expect you to believe it because I didn't do *that* either."

I look at Rad, but her eyes are fixed on her target. "Bullshit," she says. "You told Nikki you did. You told everyone you did."

"Everyone assumed I did, and I didn't stop them. Wallace's was a sweet hack, whoever did it. I *wished* I'd done it. Until now. Until all those pictures and the card deck came out. Most of all when I found out about Nikki's photos. And the comments—damn. I wanted to call her and tell her it wasn't me, but I didn't know what to say. I didn't think she'd believe me either."

Rad swats the back of his head. "Of course she wouldn't, you Gamergate ass hat. I'm not sure why I would either."

130

"'Cause it's the truth."

Rad looks away from him, at me, then back at him. "Then who did this?"

"No clue. There are probably ten hackers at school who could have done it. And another fifty at other schools who might have done it as a prank."

"Fine," I tell him. "Who cares who's doing it? Wanna prove you're a good hacker? Make things right by making sure whoever's doing this stops now. Before anyone else has their sexts sprayed across the Web."

"I was *trying* to do that when you cut off my Internet."

Haven walks over to the cable box and plugs everything back in. "I'll keep trying," he says, "but I've been working on it for hours, and there's no way to stop it. There must have been some kind of design flaw built into the Prep for Today app, and when we all put it on our phones, it started recording everything we typed."

"Like the Knock List?" Rad asks.

"That was just a tiny part of it," Haven says. "After the search-term file was discovered, someone dug further and figured out it was just the beginning of what had been recorded by Prep for Today. They must have found *all* the files."

I feel sick. "How long has the app been recording us?" I ask.

"We all installed it last spring," Haven says. "It's probably been acting as malware the entire time. You should both delete it right now."

Rad and I look at each other, worried, then immediately reach into our pockets and dump the school's scheduling app from our phones.

Rad looks back at Haven. "How do we stop them?"

"Honestly, there's nothing we can do until the hacker decides to stop."

"Can't you shut down the stupid website or something?" I ask.

"They'd just move the data set to another one. The hacker had already knocked it over to another site—Prepformore.com. Not exactly subtle. Whoever's controlling the files now has everything, I think. They could keep doing this until everyone at school's data is out there. Yours, yours, mine. Everyone's."

Rad and I leave Haven's an hour later with no better understanding of how this happened. Rad still doesn't 100 percent believe Haven isn't responsible for the leak, but if he's putting on a show, it's a damn good one. He seems genuinely broken up about what's happened to Nikki. We made him leave her a long voice mail, apologizing for taking credit for what's quickly becoming our shared nightmare. My stomach is starting to turn—something is very wrong.

"Should we go back and check on her?" Rad asks when we're back in the car.

"I think she wants space now."

"Do you want to come over?" Rad asks. "Stay over?"

"I, uh . . ."

"Forget it."

She doesn't want to be alone. She doesn't want to have to lie in her bed and think about her role in all this, and I don't want to abandon her right now. But I've been more and more nauseous since the moment Haven said this could get *bigger*. Since the moment he told us we could *all* get hit. Right now what I need is some time alone. To look through my own—apparently already hacked—phone. Alone.

"Honestly, I'm just wiped from today," I say grimly.

"Fine. Suck it, whatever. Just drive me home."

"Listen to me," I say. "This isn't your fault. Having sex was Nikki's choice, but her doing that did not in *any way* give Mattie permission to take invasive, rapey photos. This is literally no one's fault but his."

Rad looks at me. Her eyes are sad and grateful.

By the time we get to her house in Fairfax, I'm exhausted from the panic I'm suppressing. And, as much as I want to comfort her, I'm also dying to get her out of my car before she sees something's wrong with me.

Words and phrases have been popping back into my mind the entire ride: *Alkie. Ugly. Dumb.* And more. So much more. Things I don't want to believe I could have written or said. But I'm more and more sure that they're on my phone, proof that I did.

Rad takes a breath as she steps out. "Eizenberg's name will be plastered all over the newspaper tomorrow, that little shit."

Five minutes later I pull over on the side of Pickett Road and throw up. For a few seconds I get temporary relief. There's Listerine in the glove compartment (welcome to my SAD life), so I swish it around in my mouth until it hurts.

I take out my phone.

I have to call Palmer.

I hit the number with a shaking finger. He still hasn't said a word in response to my text asking if he's okay. There's no ring. Phone's off. It goes straight to voice mail, and I hear his voice for the first time in weeks.

It's Palmer. Do your thing.

Beep. Now I do my best impression of a normal person. Except my voice is the wrong pitch, and I've forgotten how to breathe while speaking.

It's me. . . . I hope you got my text. . . . I hope you're okay. . . . Look, I know you're going through some bad stuff. I'm sorry. It blows. But I need you to do something for me. If you ever gave a shit about me, I need you to delete all our texts, chats, all our DMs, everything. Please, don't even look at it. Just clear all our conversations. I don't know if this will do either of us any good, honestly. It might be too late already. Oh, and you should definitely delete Prep for Today. But if I were you, I'd delete my whole phone.

I hang up.

It takes me ten breaths—almost a whole minute—before I'm ready to look at my phone again. To do what I have to. Finally I go into my texts and find Palmer's name—buried pretty far down there now—and begin my thumb scroll of death.

There are literally thousands of texts back and forth between us over the course of three months. The most recent ones, obviously, are distant. Sad. The last embers of our dying fall fling. All now infused with the taint of *Was my boyfriend "juicing" when we were together?* Only right now, Palmer's the least of my problems.

As I scroll back, the texts get lighter. Playful. I'm not that bad at banter. For the last couple of months of my relationship with Palmer—all of November and most of December—there's hardly anything I can't live with. Maybe I'd already written my friends off and things with Palmer had already begun to fray. But when I scroll further back to the texts from October, a torrent of little comments that I can never have anyone see begins. A shit storm of cruelty that could soak through every friendship I have until they're covered in mold and have to be thrown out like a forgotten beach towel.

I keep scrolling. By late September, my bitchiness is coming in like Vin Diesel: fast and furious. There's plenty popping up on my screen that the boys could hang me with, but it's the girls I saved my deadliest venom for. Take Nikki:

> Really annoying me with all her ?s
> Shitty taste in music, don't want to go with her to some crappy show
> Scarfed down two ice cream sandwiches, then bitched abt weight 1 hr
> Always needs to be peacemaker, she'd hate if rad and I got along again, because then what role would she play?
> Nikki's mom is a disaster, total alkie. Boxed chardonnay. Her stepdad is some wall st. creep.

Why do I have to go see the play? She's only on stage crew.
Least flattering profile pic, what do I say?

And peppered everywhere, of course, Rad:

Honestly I think rad's just jealous of us
She is a total c u next tuesday sometimes
Don't care if we never talk again
Sleeps with so many cuz no self-respect
Seriously pissing me off
We're just not the same kind of people
Been to India once, thinks she's miss Bollywood
Doesn't even speak Hindi
So bitchy. Fuck her.
More notches on her bed than likes.
You don't think Rad's hot, do you?
Making our other friends choose. Such a bitch.

Not everything I wrote to Palmer about my friends makes me seem like the worst person alive. Just *almost* everything. I scream as loud as I can, half expecting the windows to shatter. It's a piercing *Walking Dead*–level scream.

How could I write these things?

Was I trying to impress a boyfriend who was out of my league? Lashing out to Palmer because I needed to blame someone else for ditching my friendships? Both? Does that excuse me saying Nikki's mother is an alcoholic—mocking her for the thing she is most unhappy about in the world?

Then there's Rad.

I scroll up and down the screen, searching for more horrible things. More betrayals. The bitchy comments, Rad could deal with, I know. She'd probably like them. Even the slutty stuff. She's said worse to my face. She might lash out, but that stuff'll pass. The stuff about her Indian-ness, that'll be a little harder to swallow.

As I scroll, my eye falls on the worst of them:

Rad's the most over the top writer on the paper, how is she editor?
Thinks she's gonna run the Washington Post someday. Only thing she can run is all her stupid sentences together.
Not half as smart as she thinks she is. Kinda dumb, actually.

Rad's always been worried that she's a fake when it comes to writing; one time she told me her deepest fear was that when you stripped away the cursing and the *I don't give a flying* attitude, people would eventually realize she's not that smart or that funny on the page or in person. Or, worse—that people *already* know. My off-the-cuff texts will be all the proof she needs. And she'll never forgive me or speak to me again. Never mind that Rad's one of the funniest, smartest people I've ever known. Just in case there was any hope left of Rad forgiving me, ever, now I'm reading an old message to Palmer detailing all the reasons why all throughout my ten-year friendship with Rad, I should've realized we were *never supposed to be friends.*

I literally listed them as bullet points! And the award for Jerk of the Century goes to Anna Soler for:

> You have no idea how much rad uses SAT words she doesn't know to try to seem smart. The college board knows all, though. 560 on the verbal. Yikes.

What the hell did I think—that Palmer and I were going to be together forever and I would never need friends again? The insanity of it is so obvious now—even Palmer was telling me it couldn't have been *all* bad if we were friends for so long. But I needed to vent. I needed to be so, so witty and so much better than my friends, who would never in a million years write that to a boy about me. I mean, probably not.

I drop my head onto the steering wheel. A sad, tiny beep comes from the horn.

And to think I was worried that Rad would find out about Jethro.

My phone vibrates.

Palmer.

I blink, reading it over and over again.

> Done. Deleted. And I'm sorry. For everything. —P

13

WHEN I WALK IN THE DOOR OF MY HOUSE, MY MOM IS SITTING at the dining room table, paying bills over a glass of white wine.

"Come talk to me, Anna," she says as I try gliding by.

I yawn for effect. "Mom, I'm really tired. Can we talk in the morning?"

"Headmaster Nichols called, sweetheart."

The concern in her eyes pierces my insides. I sit down next to her. I don't know if it's her maternal-instinct magic or if I just really need someone who loves me unconditionally, but next thing I know, I'm tearing up and telling her everything that happened—about Wallace and Palmer and Nikki. I skip the part about Jethro, though. I don't even want to think about it myself, let alone share it.

Mom takes it all in, and I can tell she's trying to contain

her outrage. At the school and their stupid app. At Mattie Eizenberg. At whoever the hacker is.

When she finally speaks, she says, "Anna, honey . . . I'm sorry I have to ask. . . . Is there anything about *you* on there? If there is . . . we'd figure it out together. We wouldn't have to tell your dad."

It. What Southern lady could even get those words out? *Naked selfie? Sexting?*

"I'm safe," I tell her, blushing.

Only now do I realize Mom's been holding her breath since she posed the question. "Yes. Of course you are."

As I start for the stairs, she adds, "I can schedule an extra session with Dr. Bechdel this week . . . if you want. You could go tomorrow. Take the morning off?"

I muster a smile. The idea of not going to school tomorrow morning is so delicious, I can taste it. But it feels important to be there for Nikki and for Rad. To finally show up when my friends need me.

"Thanks, Mom," I say. "I'm okay, though. Really."

When I'm upstairs, I think about calling Jethro. Just to check in. To hear his voice. But upset, middle-of-the-night calls send messages. Mixed messages.

Better not.

The first thing I see when I pull off Route 50, onto the main drag where Prep sits, are the vans. It's 7:45 a.m., and three or four local news vans are lined up at some kind of obviously enforced distance from school. I crack my windows and catch snippets of makeup-caked reporters rattling off words like *Sony* and *Ashley Madison*. It's cold out, and I don't want to hear more, so I roll them back up.

Prep has enough kids with parents who work inside the Beltway to make this *actual* news, and Mom and Dad and I already watched some of it this morning over pancakes they made to cheer me up. I try to breathe steadily and keep my heart rate down—rows of cameras are exactly what I don't need after last night.

Kids are milling outside their cars, gathered in clusters, sitting on one another's bumpers, waiting for *something* else to happen.

I park my car as far out as possible. I'm second-guessing my decision to turn down my mom's offer and push through it. The idea of seeing my friends' faces and having to pretend like I'm not the horrible person I seem to be in my texts and DMs is making my stomach churn. But I *have* to pretend. I can't abandon Nikki and Rad now.

Rad's car—surprise, surprise—is at the front of the lot, and she's perched on the hood. She's in full-on journalist mode, pen behind her ear, alternating between taking pictures and jotting down notes on her cell. Anybody who wants to enter any of Prep's major buildings will have to pass her 1996 Volvo to do so. Andrew is sprawled out in the passenger seat, drool pooling on his Prep varsity lacrosse jacket.

It's a relief to see a familiar face in the sea of paparazzi. "Hey. Did you talk to Nik this morning?"

Rad twirls the pen, then sticks it behind her ear. A good night's sleep has brought some of her mojo back. "Stopped by on the way. She's eighty-sixing herself for the day."

"Haven?"

"No way. Everyone still thinks he did it, and they've already got things he *actually* did earlier in the year that Nichols could get him on. Dude's a ghost, at least till his dad comes home."

From the Reddit threads, I know Haven's a split decision. A lot of people are furious, obviously. But many of those who haven't been hurt LOVE Haven because they think he knocked the little princes and princesses off their thrones.

I bump Rad's hip, and she scooches over to make room for me on the car hood. "How long have you been here?"

"I was out of my house by six-fifteen, picked up that bozo"—she indicates Andrew with her thumb—"and was here by six-forty-five."

I nod at Andrew and whisper, "He must really like you if he skipped his wake 'n' bake to come with you at six a.m."

"He didn't skip it," Rad says. "He squeezed it in on the ride over. I think he should cool it on the weed, though. You should've heard the conspiracy theories."

"And Jethro didn't want a front-row seat with you guys?"

"Think he's helping Haven figure out who's doing it."

"You know what?" Andrew pipes up from the passenger seat. "I bet Eizenberg doesn't even show his face today. His parents prolly filed transfer papers already. It's really too bad, because I was planning on kicking his ass next time I see him. My current thinking is, he needs the word *rapist* carved into his forehead."

Suddenly a voice, booming yet faraway-sounding, comes from inside Rad's Volvo. "Ladies and gentlemen, the moment you've all been waiting for!"

I peer back at Andrew through the windshield. He's not talking. Confused, I crane my neck to look in the backseat. Did I miss someone? Nope, empty.

Then I spot the iPad on Andrew's lap, which has a cable running to the car stereo. "Drum roll, please," the voice says through the speakers. To my surprise, kids all around me start slapping their palms against their thighs, their stomachs, their notebooks, the roofs and dashboards of their cars. Cars have their doors open, and the same voice is coming from every stereo. The effect is eerie, unsettling.

"Who's talking?" I ask Rad.

She holds up a palm. "Just listen."

"Thank you, thank you very much," says the voice, cornpone Elvis-style. Then, in a normal voice, "This is Timmy Tepper, reporting to you live from somewhere very very close by Alexandria Preparatory Academy. Live, I repeat, live. This is a live stream, not taped. I have eyes and ears in the Prep parking lot, and their mouths—well, mostly fingers—are telling me what is going down. And right now I'm hearing that the first of the Instagram Six has arrived! Joshy Klein!"

Rad hops off the hood, onto the ground, to get a closer look.

There are stray claps and hoots throughout the parking lot as the door to a Jetta pops open on the north side. Josh Klein—of AP-exam cheating fame—steps out and tries to pretend he isn't being watched. Josh rides the bench on the baseball team, and this morning he has his white base-ball cap pulled extremely low.

Tepper's voice booms through again as Josh hurries to-ward the front door. "Josh, tell us, where can the *rest* of us buy a hat that can be pulled so low? It's not so great for going incognito, like you were desperately hoping to do, but it *is* the *perfect* hat for cheating your way through just about any class!"

"Who is Timmy Tepper?" I ask.

Rad says, "Remember that scrawny redhead dude Wal-lace was torturing in the dining hall the day after win-ter break? *That's* Timmy. Guess he does some nerdy Prep sports podcast, so he had everything in place already, the lucky little shit. He had the stream up and running *be-fore sundown* last night. Admin won't let him broadcast on campus, but they can't stop him either. He has free speech on his side—his dad is some kinda constitutional lawyer."

Josh opens the front door and finally disappears into the temporary sanctuary of the school lobby. The mood in the parking lot is gleeful. Everyone loves watching these Instas fall so hard.

While he waits for the next arrival, Timmy goes into marketing mode. "Welcome to the twenty-teens, people. Those of you who missed yesterday's live stream, where we covered every inch of every playing card in Mattie Ei-zenberg's deck, can now download it on iTunes and Au-dible."

I shudder to think about Nikki listening to that pod-cast, and I turn to Rad. "We'll get Haven or Jethro to find a way to take it down."

Rad shakes her head, a hint of sadness spreading across her face amid all the excitement. "What's the point?"

"So Nik doesn't have to hear herself ridiculed?"

"Someone already made a collage and put up everyone who's over eighteen on RedTube. Like, a million hits already." I can hear the anger in Rad's voice.

"Oh my, loyal listeners," Timmy roars. "Do we have a treat for you. Let's call it . . . *two studs, one car.*"

I turn my head in the same direction as everybody else's. And there, as promised, is Dylan, stepping out of the driver's seat of his black Jeep Cherokee. Immediate laughter and snickering and catcalls rise up from all sides of the parking lot.

Timmy: "For the first, hold the *u*! That spells *STD*, for those of you who flubbed the verbal section. Mr. Dylan Johnson, ladies and gentlemen!"

Someone offers up one of those wolf whistles people do to catch a taxi, and people laugh. But soon it becomes clear that Dylan and his johnson are just the appetizer for this hungry crowd. The Jeep's passenger door swings open, and Palmer steps to the ground. It's the first time I've seen him since the basketball game. He still hasn't texted anything more after our one exchange.

"And now," Timmy announces, "stud number *deux*. Stud indeed, people. Do you know they make racehorses piss before the Triple Crown to make sure they haven't been doped? Has the *recently single* Palmer Meade, who already looks like he belongs on a Wheaties box, been taking more than just Wheaties to recover from his injury?"

Palmer reaches into the car and pulls his green canvas

bag onto his back using both straps, as always. I told him once that when he combines his bag with his aviator glasses, like he has today, he looks like he's headed to Fallujah.

"Every day of high school is a battle, soldier," he'd replied.

Something tightens in my chest, thinking about it now. Despite everything, I feel terrible for him. I can't read his face, but I know he doesn't deserve this.

As Palmer begins his walk of whatever he's feeling right now beneath those glasses, Timmy comes booming back in. "For those playing along at home, we took a Survey-Monkey late last night to find out what you all believe, and the results are in: ninety-two percent of you think that the balls of our favorite corn-fed dribbler are the size of kernels!"

I could assure everyone this isn't true, but it doesn't seem like the time. Especially since Palmer is walking right by Rad's Volvo. His first post-juicing-story appearance.

As he passes by us, he takes off his sunglasses and looks right in my direction. His eyes are dry. But it's the closest I've ever come to seeing Palmer tear up, and I freeze dead still. And suddenly I'm very afraid for him: 92 percent of Prep may be too quick to believe rumors they read in a text exchange, but this time I think they may be right. I can only imagine what he's feeling right now: he must be in danger of being kicked off the team or of being suspended, the NCAA is probably hot on his heels, and he could lose his chance at Duke.

Hey, Palmer mouths without any sound.

I wonder if he's been able to sleep at all. His hands are in his pockets, but I bet his fingernails are chewed raw, which happened when things got bad before.

I'm about to respond with my own *Hey* when Rad tells him, "Get lost, 'roid head. Anna's closed for business."

"Rad . . ."

But Rad shoots me back a look of death. Conversation over. I'm caught between a best friend I'm walking on eggshells around and the ex-boyfriend I'm starting to feel real sorry for, God knows why. It's lose-lose for this loser.

Palmer puts his sunglasses back on and makes his way into the building.

I don't want to get into it with Rad, and for the first time, Timmy Tepper's voice feels like a welcome distraction: "And, speak of the devil who wears Prada," he narrates, "the ace of spades in the deck: it's Prep's own Vanessa Euuuubanks!"

A hush falls over the crowd as Vanessa makes her way across the parking lot. She's in a white knit dress that ends midthigh, black high heels, and enormous sunglasses, her blond hair pulled back in a ponytail. It's an outfit that screams HONEY BADGER DON'T GIVE A DAMN. She's not doing a perp walk, like Josh and her ex Dylan did.

Even Tepper respects for a moment before finally chiming in again. "Yesterday, Vanessa Eubanks, the girl you love to hate, or at least the girl you'd love to hate-fudge—this a family show, folks—the girl who hooked up with Dylan for about five minutes fall semester when it looked like Palmer was lovey-dovey with Anna Soler for the long haul, was seen entering a nearby LabCorp yesterday afternoon with, a reliable source reports, a very concerned expression on her face."

But from the look on Vanessa's face, you'd think she couldn't hear a word Timmy's saying, even though it's blasting from every speaker in the parking lot. She's giving a master class in holding your head high. Then, just as Vanessa's about to pass Rad's car, she pauses and, pivoting gracefully on one very high heel, lets her sunglasses slide down the bridge of her nose. She looks right at Rad.

"You're the editor of the newspaper, right?"

Rad, unflappable Rad, swallows audibly, makes an actual cartoon-character gulping noise, before saying in a reasonably cool tone, "Yeah."

"Your next headline." Vanessa drops a crumpled slip of paper on Rad's lap, then makes a second graceful pivot and disappears inside Ewing.

"Hell is it?" Andrew asks.

Rad studies the paper. "I think it's a blood test."

"Why would Vanessa give you her blood test?" I ask.

Rad guffaws. "She's controlling the narrative. She's herpes-free. Totally clean. And she wants me to print it in the *Xandria*."

First period on Tuesdays, I have a double block of PE (the price of not playing any sports at Prep), which is a pretty weird way to start the first day of school in a post-deck-of-cards world. Of the nine girls in my class, two of them were in Mattie's deck. So, even though I haven't looked at the cards or pics beyond what Rad showed me at chapel,

I have seen Erin Green and Deirdre Nikzad in the buff before.

As Mr. Fortini feebly attempts to teach a bunch of nonathletes the rules of badminton, a funny thing happens. Everyone is actually being nice to Erin and Deirdre. The boys smile gently but don't gawk at what they already know is beneath the girls' gym clothes, and the other girls are extra cool. There aren't any catty comments—or comments at all. One of the band boys says *Sucks, sorry*, to Erin genuinely as we break to go back to the locker rooms, but that's about it. Maybe it's because Erin and Deirdre aren't Instagrams, and—like Nikki—they didn't have *anything* coming to them.

I go to third period in a slightly better mood and text Nikki to tell her. An hour of hitting around those stupid birdies has actually given me a tiny bit of hope. Maybe Vanessa is acceptable collateral damage 'cause Vanessa is Vanessa.

Sadly not.

You know that whiny book they make you read in sophomore lit? *Candide?* It's by that French philosopher, and the moral of the story seems to be, optimism is for idiots. Well, the rest of my day seems to prove his point.

Gym was a fluke. The exception.

Each new period I go to, there's more whispering, more kids not in class because they've been so horribly humiliated that they've gone home or they are in Nichols's office being interrogated. Every period things get worse—more gossip spreads by the hour, and Prep kids are in an arms race to see who can spread it in the most amusing, viral way. Some people post stuff on their own feeds, but 4chan and Yik Yak are blowing up too; the trolls are using them to make their nastiest posts anonymously. And we're all sneaking looks at our phones between periods, lots of people even during class.

As I head to sixth period, history with Mr. Kisker—the only class I share with Jethro—I'm nervous, of course. When I walk in, Jethro's in his usual seat in the last row, but he doesn't look anywhere in my direction. It's the first time I've seen him since chapel yesterday, and he's just staring at his computer screen.

"This is a media-history class," Kisker says as I slip into my seat. "And, given that we have news trucks sitting a hundred yards from Prep today, I'd like nothing more than to discuss what's happened. But we are going to hold off until we have more information. Until there is something concrete. So let's return to where we ended yesterday. As I was saying, no one has handled *and* mishandled the media better than O. J. Simpson."

I spend most of the period watching Jethro instead of the images from O.*J.: Trial of the Century* on my monitor. A couple of times I try to get his attention, but it's becoming increasingly clear that he's ignoring me now. Maybe he was just putting on a show, but yesterday it seemed like he was genuinely moving on from the other night. That he'd forgiven me for being . . . reckless with his feelings. Or at least indecisive about my own. He was even pretty nice about the Palmer stuff, even though I know hearing that name must make him sick.

The more Jethro ignores me, the more I want him to look at me. Typical. When things are easy, I don't pay as much attention to him as I should. But when things are bad in my life, I *need* him bad. And right now I want to make eye contact with him, to give him a look so that he knows I want to connect with him. I want him to tap on the doorsill in a way that tells me everything is going to be okay.

Am I actually in love with him?

Do I just like having him be in love with me?

God, I'm a mess.

The seventh-period bell rings, and Jethro rushes out of class. He doesn't even glance in my direction.

I know he has BC calculus next, and he's pulling books from the top shelf of his locker as I approach. Finally we make eye contact. Finally.

"Hey," I say as his locker neighbor heads off. "Are you okay?"

Jethro turns. Takes a long breath before saying, "Not really."

"What's wrong?"

"Other than everything?"

"I mean . . . why were you ignoring me in class?"

"I wasn't."

"Are we . . . still okay?"

"Not everything is about you, Anna."

I step back a little. There's an edge in his voice that I don't recognize but probably deserve. It stings, either way. "Uh. Okay. Forget it. Sorry I asked."

I turn and start to walk away, feeling the uninvited knot in my throat.

"Wait," Jethro says. "Anna. Hey. Stop. I'm sorry. It's just . . ."

I turn slowly.

He leans his head toward mine. "I just mean, I can't believe it's happening like this," he whispers. "It's so bad, Anna. It was funny for a second, when it was Wallace. But Nikki and all the rest of them? Everyone is fighting over text messages from, like, months ago. We're all losing our damn minds. Know what I heard in chem? Bobby Simkins said he was going to kill Aiden Murphy for some DM he sent one of the Instagrams. And honestly, knowing Bobby Simkins, I think he might."

I shake my head. "Do you think you and Haven can find the person who leaked everything? So it'll stop?"

"I've got even heavier hitters helping," he says. "Some college dudes at Johns Hopkins, old mathlete guys." Jethro's eyes are already red, and he rubs them for a second. "And we're not trying to find the person. We're trying to find the *people*."

"There's more than one?"

He nods.

"Like . . . some sort of—what? A bunch of hackers working together?"

"No, that's the thing," Jethro says. "There's no collective here. No Anonymous or fsociety or anything else. No one's working together."

"I don't understand. How do you even know that?"

He kicks his locker softly. "Whoever did the Wallace

leak is different from whoever did yesterday's with the other Instagrams."

"What do you mean?"

He takes a big breath. "It's complicated, but from the way it looks, the first hacker probably just wanted Wallace. No harm, no foul. Even Haven wanted to take credit. But then other hackers saw the way into the enormous cache of Prep for Today files, and they made copies of the data set. Plus, you've seen how many trolls are reposting everything. It doesn't matter who started it now. All that matters is, there's no stopping it."

The third floor of Dwight Library is normally my place to escape. No one else likes the third-floor bathroom 'cause there's only one stall and it smells weird. I like it because no one else likes it. I need a moment to panic in private. Desperately. Because now I know: it's just a matter of time before my stuff is leaked.

Unfortunately, the third-floor bathroom ain't empty today. It doesn't smell any better than usual, but there is a pair of ballet flats at the bottom of the sole stall. As the door closes behind me with a heavy clang, there are scrambling noises, and then I hear something light and metal land on the floor.

A razor blade, fresh blood on the edge.

A hand quickly snatches it up. Oh Jesus. I don't know if I should try to leave before whoever's in there comes out. Or tell some well-meaning guidance counselor. Or stay and act like I haven't noticed anything.

Before I can decide, the stall door swings open.

It's Hannah Moyer, a junior lacrosse player who I know a little through Andrew. She's yanking down both sleeves of her sweater. I haven't heard anything about her in the leaks; as far as I know, Hannah's not in Mattie's.

"Hey," I say.

She fixes her short, cropped black hair, brushing it over like she just stepped out of a convertible. "Hey."

"You okay?" I ask, unable to stop myself.

Hannah stares at me for five awkward seconds. Finally she says, "Would you be? Everyone thinks that I'm crazy now. Suicidal."

I take a breath before I react, because I don't want to say anything bad. I knew a couple of kids like her at Silver Pines, and the crazy thing is, most cutters aren't suicidal. They're just . . . in pain. And need *more*, or, like, a different kind.

Hannah moves to the mirror to fix her mascara. "Batshit cray, halfway to Bathtubville," she continues. "*Prepare your funeral speech, Brian*. That's what she wrote. On stupid Twitch."

Twitch is a random gaming-video site I thought only trolls went on. I didn't even know anyone with two X chromosomes was *allowed* to go on it. The Brian in question is a sophomore—sciency guy, I think?—who Hannah's hung out with on and off.

I look at Hannah in the mirror. "Who said that to Brian?" I ask.

She grabs a handful of tissues and shuts herself back in the stall. "Colleen. Our families go to the Outer Banks together. We talked about applying to the same colleges. She's supposed to be one of my best friends."

After the last bell, I keep my head down. I don't want to have anything to do with other people's business. It's not easy. In a corner of the senior lounge, Martha Stevenson's talking in hushed tones with Jill Fay about comments on her "rank" body odor, made to one of the Instas; outside the snack bar, the hockey goalie is pulling apart two best puckheads forever over gross stuff one snapped about the other's girlfriend. *I'd muff dive on that whale like Jules Verne, yo,* didn't go over very well with the boyfriend, apparently. It doesn't help that someone's already Auto-Tuned it and put it up on YouTube.

Who am I to judge? And how long do I have until my idiotic, off-the-cuff, *I am undeserving of the company of civilized humans* comments about *my* best friends, which could send any one of them into a Hannah-like spin, get leaked?

It sounds narcissistic, I know. Especially after what Nikki, Palmer, and others have been through. They've had it so rough, and here I am worrying about what awful thing *might possibly* happen to me if and when my phone gets leaked. Only, I can't help it. Just when my friends have come around to forgiving me, they'll realize that I'm not just a friend abandoner who didn't even have the decency to choose chicks over dicks, but *also* an evil, gossiping jerk. Standing at my locker, I hold my phone out of sight in case any teachers walk by. Group text to Rad and Nikki: *Can we hang later, please?* I hit Send and wait. I take a long swig from my water bottle, trying to cool myself down. I need to know things are okay. I need to know that nothing of mine has been let out of the bottle and that Nikki isn't sitting at home, realizing that I'm the worst. That Rad isn't in her car, preparing to mow me down when I walk out the doors.

The halls are practically empty now. Usually people linger after school, but the leaks have everyone running to their cars and home to their devices to see what else has been leaked/discovered/trolled.

I wait. And wait.

Nothing.

I slip my phone back in my pocket. I burrow my head in my locker. What would Dr. Bechdel tell me in this moment? Probably to have "presence of mind." Okay. Here's how my mind feels in the present: vulnerable. I need some confirmation that my friends are still in touch with me, that they still have my back.

I down every drop from the water bottle to distract myself, and now I think I have to pee. But the bathroom near my locker doesn't have good cell service. What if I miss their texts?

Oh, come on, Anna.

Suddenly I hear a voice. "'Sup, Anna? You trying to climb inside your locker?"

Some kid in our grade I don't really know but I think is named Ralph walks by and smiles awkwardly at me. "What? No . . ."

"Hope Meade never 'roid raged on you," he says. "Heard

they're making him piss in a cup before he can play in the next game. Whoops. Sayonara, Duke!"

"Don't be an asshole," I say. He shrugs and walks down the hall.

Five minutes later, neither of my girls has said a word back.

I send myself a text to make sure it's working. It pops back immediately. *Test text*. There's no technical glitch. I stare at the screen inside the open locker. Checking the bars to make sure I have service. Turning the ringer on and off. Everything's working.

My heart beats faster and faster. Group text number two:

Nik—is your mom going out? We'll come over. Right, R?

Freshman and sophomore year, if thirty seconds went by and I didn't get a response from one of them, I would've worried that they must have been in a gruesome car accident together and I needed to call the cops. But from the time our parents let us get phones, that *never* happened. Even as my anxiety issues got worse before Silver Pines, I'd always respond to Nikki and Rad immediately, even if it was just our code for why we couldn't talk: *SSSS*—"Stupid shit, soul sister."

Now it's been ten minutes and two unanswered texts.

I can't resist now. I go onto my browser and go to Prepforevenmorebitches.com—the URL changed again after the school IT staff got the last one shut down. I search the page, my eyes tripping over the heap of gossip.

There's nothing more about me—nothing new.

I feel like I'm crazed and paranoid. Waiting to be busted.

I head to the art lab and try to work on my selfie portrait's chin.

It's tempting to give myself a new one in the painting, since my real chin has a slight point I've always hated. I'm trying to embrace it, though. Kyle Cherski is the only other kid in here, and Mr. Touhey isn't a stickler about the phone thing, but he does believe our screens distract us.

I sneak looks in my pocket every few minutes. I keep imagining that my phone is vibrating. The show is just over a week away now, and I should be thinking about the fact that my selfie self-portrait is nowhere near finished. The only thing that's certain is that it isn't very good, and I don't know how to fix it.

Then it happens. My phone vibrates.

I don't know whether to be excited or terrified.

Then I reach into my pocket, and I realize—the vibration is much longer than it should be. This is the vibration of a *call*.

The screen confirms it. It's Rad. CALLING ME. Like, actually calling me, with no warning. I can't remember the last time she called me without texting me first.

Calling is rarely a good sign. Also, I hate talking on the phone.

I nod at Kyle on my way out of the art lab. "Hey," I

whisper into the phone once I'm in the hallway. Then, as casually as I can: "What's up?"

Rad takes a long, dramatic breath. I can feel her gearing up for a bigger ass whipping than Gwen gave Gavin when sexts to a family iPad gave him and the nanny away.

"Yo, I need you at Haven's," Rad says.

I look down the empty stairwell outside the art lab. Staring into the abyss. Has there been another leak? Did I miss it on the site? Is my data out? Is Palmer's? Are they all going to pile on and crucify me? Will I walk into one of those *To Catch a Predator*-like interventions/public shaming sessions if I actually show up at Haven's?

"Right now? I'm in the art lab."

"Anna, if you ever want to be my friend again, get your ass over to Haven's right now. With the damn Nikon. I'll be there in ten minutes. We have to make sure he's okay and find out exactly what happened. People need to know. We're putting it all in the *Xandria* tomorrow."

"I don't . . . what happened?"

"The cops went to his house. In SWAT gear."

I push the phone toward my ear. Could I have heard her right? "The cops showed up for Haven? Isn't that a little extreme, even for Nichols? I—"

Rad interrupts me. "They weren't at his house investigating the hack. Someone called the cops and told them Haven was stockpiling guns and planning a school shooting or something insane like that."

It's hard not to scream. "Haven would never do that!"

"Of course not," Rad says. "Someone SWATed him,

Anna. Some troll did it to punish him for what's happening. Anyway, they showed up in riot gear. Haven's dad tried to stop them from coming in without a warrant, and the SWAT team pinned him to the ground and arrested him. Haven is scared shitless."

14

You might think a house that's just been stormed by a SWAT team would look a certain way—windows and doors thrown open or smashed and off hinges, furniture thrown about the yard, everything torn apart from the inside out—but as I pull up Haven's driveway, the place looks no different from last night. Even the trash cans have been righted and emptied, lined up neatly along the fence.

But, unlike last night, there's no need to smoke out this fox. Haven's already outside, sitting on the front steps, head in his hands. My heart skips a little, but more in the holding-back-tears way than from actual palpitations. He's probably been out here since they took his dad, and he watched his only parent get cuffed and stuffed into a van.

As I shut my door, headlights pull in behind me. Haven finally looks up. His face is pale, and the red around his eyes is worse than usual. I take a deep breath so I don't break down. What good is a supportive friend who can't keep her own shit together? I give him a little wave and he half smiles, patting the stair next to him. We don't say anything; we just wait in silence as Rad cuts her engine and the lights dim.

I feel Haven's whole body tense before I see that Rad isn't alone.

Nikki trails a step behind her as they approach.

Nikki says, "Hi, guys," her voice barely above a whisper.

It seems to trigger something in Haven, because he literally leaps from the step, his skinny body uncoiling like a spring, and wraps Nikki in a big hug.

I hear a muffled, "I'm so sorry, Nik."

Nikki wipes at her eyes as the two of them pull apart. "I know. I know it wasn't you."

"I'm gonna find out who did this, I swear," he says. "And if Mattie's dumb enough to show his face in school tomorrow, I'll kill him."

Nikki groans, "No more death threats, please."

"Besides, Mattie deserves a fate worse than death," I say, linking my arm through Nik's.

"For real," Rad agrees. "Like, something medieval—oh, or that bottomless chair in *Casino Royale*."

Haven shudders noticeably.

"Perfect," Nikki says. She leans her head on Rad's shoulder.

Nikki turns to him. "Wait, you're coming to school tomorrow? How?"

Haven shakes his head. "Not sure. My dad called right before you guys got here. He should be released soon, just

162

finishing up the paperwork—he's so pissed. I guess there's an emergency Prep parents' meeting tonight. He's going there to tell Nichols it wasn't me. To clear my name. Said he can prove it. And I can't miss any more school or I'll lose my spot at MIT."

"How can he prove it?" I ask.

Haven grimaces. "I don't know. Especially since he's been away for a week. Whatever it is, I don't care. Just as long as he helps me get out of this."

"What time's the meeting?" Rad asks.

"It's parents only, Rad," Nikki says.

Rad shrugs it off. "Doesn't matter. We need to find out what's going on, if Haven really *is* safe to go back tomorrow." When we all hesitate, she adds, "It's basically a matter of life and death."

"I'm in enough trouble as it is," Haven says.

"I'll stay here," Nikki says, putting her arm around Haven.

Before I can come up with an excuse or important task for myself (aka *not* trespassing on school property and spying on a bunch of powerful adults), Rad says, "Looks like it's you and me, Anna."

"Not gonna lie," I say. "This sounds like an awful idea."

"See you there at seven-oh-five sharp" is all she says.

On the drive to the school, I call my therapist. Tonight, alone in my car, on the way to breaking into my high school, feels like the right time.

"It would suck for anyone, Anna," Dr. Bechdel is saying.

"Anyone. Even beyond what's happened to your friends, it's such a major invasion of privacy. Does it make you worry that your own information could be leaked?"

I take a deep breath. "Terrified."

Talking to Dr. Bechdel instantly unseals something in me that I usually keep closed. She's so calm and nonjudgmental. It feels really safe.

"Have you been following it all on tweets?" she asks.

I also love how adorably untechie she is.

"Just lurking a bit, but I haven't posted anything."

"It's natural that you're curious. Anyone would be. I think it's important to try to keep what you see in perspective, though. Try to remember, what you see on there is not the whole story. It's no one's whole reality."

Another nice thing about Dr. Bechdel is that she never speaks in absolutes; she doesn't chide you for being like everyone else. She preaches moderation.

"Let's talk more about it at our next session," she continues. "Until then, *breathe*. Remember our exercises. And you can always take a Xanax in an emergency. We want to wean off, but we don't need any setbacks in the process, okay?"

"Got it. Thanks."

I shared only the tip of the iceberg with Dr. Bechdel, but it felt good to hear her voice. Everything that's happened is going to take an extralong session to get through. Doing what Rad and I are about to do could take up an entire session by itself.

As I pull into school, the parking lot is dark and filled with fancy, parent cars. Rad waves me down in her all-black spy ensemble, from her black Vans to a black beret perched on her head. In silent, tennis-shoe-clad feet, I approach.

"Are you kidding me with that hat?" I whisper-laugh.

"I need to be fully in character," Rad says.

I look back at my car. "Hey, are you sure you want to do this? There's still time to turn around, maybe go to the diner."

But Rad's firm. "Anna, we're doing this. Now, get your phone out."

"I literally only have my license in my pocket. Thought anything else or anything tech would be, like, a liability or something. I don't exactly trust my phone right now."

Rad shoots me a look, straightens her beret, and walks toward the chapel.

Against my better judgment, I follow her up the back staircase to the balcony. We kneel behind one of the banisters.

The meeting's already well under way.

Headmaster Nichols is finishing his address, and I can't help but notice how sweaty he looks as he speaks to the parents. "The software—and I'm no expert here; I still type up all my speeches on my good old Olivetti—was designed to be able to record data. *But* that function was only supposed to be turned on in the event of an emergency. Unfortunately, there was a glitch in the initial code. It turned on the recording function as soon as the students installed the application on their phones."

An angry voice interrupts. "So you've been *spying* on our kids for a year?"

I crane my neck. The voice belongs to a fast-forward-thirty-years version of Jocelyn van Mecl, Wallace's ex and Vanessa's second in command.

"Certainly not," says Headmaster Nichols. "I will reiterate that the school's role in this was purely accidental. We've instructed all students to delete the app, and the board is considering taking legal action against the developer."

"Deny, deny, deny," Rad whispers, shaking her head. "Classic."

Another voice, belonging to a man in a pinstripe suit, says, "Maybe you were hoping you could blackmail our kids into making large donations when they're forty?"

A few parents laugh darkly. Headmaster Nichols ignores this one. *"As I was saying,"* he continues, "to halt the further spread of information, I'll be issuing an increased penalty for any student who goes on social media on school property. Students who are caught using it will now be automatically suspended—a serious deterrent. I would appreciate it if you would enforce this mandate at home too."

"Yeah right," another father calls out. "Our kids are tech geniuses compared with us. The measures you're taking are useless."

A mother in a Chanel suit, calfskin heels, and flawless makeup raises her hand. "Frankly, I'm eager for you to shut down the podcast of this—Tommy Tippler?"

"Timmy Tepper," Headmaster Nichols corrects.

"I love this lady's Jackie O. look," Rad murmurs.

"Whatever his name is, he needs to be stopped," Jackie O. continues. "His podcast is destructive and a menace."

Suddenly I see someone and gasp. Haven's dad is sitting in the back row of pews.

Rad elbows my ribs to keep me quiet. I point in Mr. Dodd's direction. He's a stern-looking man with the same features as Haven but a very different expression on his face.

Meanwhile, Nichols takes a handkerchief out of his pocket, blots his head and face, and says, "Timmy Tepper's father is, unfortunately, at least for us"—he lets go with an unconvincing chuckle—"an expert in constitutional law. As many of you know, we wanted to shut down the podcast. Mr. Tepper said he'd sue us. His son's podcast has never been permitted to broadcast from Prep grounds. But we can't stop him from broadcasting elsewhere."

The assembled parents let out a collective groan.

Headmaster Nichols holds up a calming hand. I think even his ears are sweating now. "Furthermore, all our efforts are focused on locating the perpetrator. I hope that until we do, you'll be patient with us."

"You mean that sociopath Haven Dodd," Mrs. van Mecl says. "Why can't you smoke him out?"

"Here we go," Rad whispers, inching her dutifully recording phone closer to the edge of the balcony.

"There is no proof that Haven Dodd had anything to do with this. What's more, earlier today, a student called in a false—and very serious—claim that Haven was planning an attack at Prep, which led to a dangerous incident with the police. Actions such as this are no better than—"

Nichols is cut short when Mr. Dodd stands at the back of the chapel.

The rest of the audience murmurs excitedly. They're just like us, I see now. Hungry for more dirt. So much for maturing as we age.

"Joe—Mr. Dodd," Nichols says. "We're glad you're here."

"My son had nothing to do with these leaks," Mr. Dodd says, his voice calm.

"Bullshit," someone calls out.

But Mr. Dodd continues, undeterred. "I know Haven didn't do this because I can prove that Jethro Stephens is responsible."

You know when you're on a bridge or rooftop with no railing and you get that weird feeling that you'll fall? Even if you're not planning to throw yourself off, it's still scary. It's like your body might betray you and spaz out, or some external force will push you. Well, right now I'm driving home, breathing as slowly as possible and trying not to let anything tip me one way or another. Trying not to crash.

The parents' meeting got out of hand after Mr. Dodd threw Jethro under the bus—no, scratch that: threw him under the freaking combine harvester. Rad sensed I was close to panic, because she eventually tucked her phone in her back pocket, squeezed my hand, and guided me back down the stairs. Rad thinks they probably have as little on Jethro as they do on Haven, which is to say nada. But something about Mr. Dodd's voice makes me wonder.

Finally I can't take it anymore.

I pull over on the side of the road and dial Jethro.

"They need a scapegoat," he says calmly after I explain what's happened.

"I'm worried, Jethro," I tell him.

"About me?"

"Well, yeah. I mean, what if the cops come for you? What about MIT?"

"Whoa, Anna, chill. Let's take it one day at a time."

"I'm sorry. I'm getting more worked up about this than you are."

"Yeah, let's back up for a sec, hold off on the anxiety till we really need it."

"Hey, I've got anxiety for days. I can share it with you anytime."

I can practically hear him smiling. "I kind of can't believe Mr. Dodd said that in front of everyone," Jethro says.

"And you didn't do it!" I say. "What do you think Mr. Dodd has?"

Jethro inhales. "I don't know. The only thing I can think of is that he caught me using Haven's computer at their house last week. We thought the place was empty. Haven went out to get takeout and left me there. Mr. Dodd walked in and saw I was finishing some stupid hack Haven started."

"What were you hacking?"

"Haven was trying to get into the mainframe of the National Zoo."

"The zoo?"

"It was a joke. He was gonna change the names of some of the donors to stupid animal names. John McMonkey. William P. Walrus. It was *so* dumb; he was just trying to see if we could do it. Mr. Dodd came home early, I took the blame. There was no point in bringing Haven down too."

"So what . . . now he's using that as his proof?"

"It doesn't look good," Jethro says, then makes some grumbling sound I can't quite decipher. I can picture him sitting on the blue-carpeted floor of his bedroom, among the comic books and vinyls, back to the frame of his wooden bed.

"Anna, listen," he tells me. "I gotta go somewhere."

"What? Where?"

"I don't know. I just need to figure some things out."

"Like, away from home? How can I reach you?"

"Just give me some time," he says. "I love you."

Those three words.

I've said them to Rad and Nikki a million times. But I've never said them to Jethro or any other boy before. I don't know exactly what they mean tonight.

"I love you too, Jethro."

Whether or not I'm *in* love with him is beside the point right now.

As I take out my keys to unlock the front door to my house, I hear footsteps rushing around inside. Then the door flies open, and Mom stares back at me—with a look I don't understand. Does she know what Rad and I just did somehow?

"I just got the mail," Mom says. "There's an envelope, Anna. From *RISD*."

My heart jumps.

I rush inside, looking around, and quickly snatch up the envelope from the dining room table. It's large. I can feel that it's full of papers. Does that mean . . . ?

"Dear Anna," I read aloud to Mom and Dad, my voice quivering. *"Thank you for your application. We are delighted to offer you a place at the Rhode Island School of Design!"* Then I see the final sentence, and my eyes well on the spot.

"Oh my God," I tell my parents. "I got a *partial scholarship.*"

They hug me; they hug each other. We sit on the couch, and Dad lets me have a little sip of his wine to celebrate. Mom kisses my head. They're so proud of me. At least now I have a way out. I'm not going to be here forever. Despite everything, I feel so lucky. For a moment, the leaks, Nikki's crying in the bathroom, the parents' meeting, even Jethro—all fall away from my mind.

Until they don't.

Once I'm alone in my bedroom, I text Rad, Nikki, Andrew, Haven, and Dr. Bechdel about getting into college. I text Jethro and tell him to call again when he can.

The girls and Andrew hit me back immediately—all super excited. Not to be self-absorbed, but it's a tiny bright spot for all of us right now, I think. I hope the rest of them get into school soon and it helps them forget about this disaster, even just for a moment.

Nothing from Haven or Jethro. Haven texted me and Rad a dozen times after he found out what happened to tell us his dad is making him keep his mouth shut or he's going to take away his phone, his computers, his car keys, everything. Without those things, he can barely live, much less help prove Jethro didn't do this.

I throw open my laptop and message Jethro.

Call me when you can.

Hours later, I can't sleep. My eyes are still glued to my laptop. There are about a dozen tabs open. Frida Kahlo slide shows—for self-portrait inspiration. O. J. Simpson–trial conspiracy-theory threads, for media-history class. Pictures of the RISD dorms and lists of classes offered, all of which excite me: Two-Dimensional Design. Color Theory.

But somehow I still can't look forward.

I keep winding up back at Prep-themed hack trolling. God, I feel gross. Gross for reading about other people but even grosser for looking for information about myself. About what other people think of me. For finding out whether my info has been posted on Prep for Whatever.

I shove my laptop away from me and feel around my bed for my pajamas. I feel something beneath my butt. I do all my work on the bed and almost never sit in this chair, so it's not surprising when I find a pair of jeans crumpled up on top of it.

I dig into the pockets, and on the right side is a lump.

Jethro's thumb drive from the first day of the semester.

It's a relief to find it right now, this little time machine that can take me back to a time before the leaks, before the sex. Back to the time before the Torpedo Factory and before I remembered all the terrible things I said about my friends.

I uncap the top to the drive, and I'm about to stick it into one of the open USB ports when I hear a series of sounds. First comes the gavel—*doink-doink*—that kicks off a *Law and Order* episode on the TV in the den, where my parents are.

But there's something else.

Is that . . . a light tapping behind me?

Someone is at my window.

I freeze. My blood goes cold.

From the shadow cast across my carpet, I can tell it's a man!

This is not how I want to die. Not yet! I had sex with only one person! One time! I didn't even get to go to RISD and see if I find myself!

"Anna! Open up. It's me."

Oh. I know that voice.

I unfreeze and slowly open my eyes. Craning my neck, I see a tall figure. His hands are cupped around his eyes, and he's peering through the glass.

Palmer.

"Thank God you live on the first floor," he says, swinging one long leg over the sill. But he pauses before swinging the other, so it looks, briefly, as if he's riding the window like a pony. "Wait, is it okay if I come in?"

"I mean technically, you're already in. But yes."

I hurry over to my door to make sure it's locked. My

dad's an easygoing guy, but he's still Colombian when it comes to boys in his daughter's bedroom. Hence the fact that this is the first time Palmer has been in here when my parents are home.

I flip the light switch on, and I get a shock when I turn back.

Palmer looks awful. I mean, awful for *him*, anyway. His face is drawn and pale, and his eyes are shadowed and pouchy, and his lips are chapped. He looks like an extra from the middle part of a disaster movie—still beautiful but visibly rattled, worn out.

Palmer grinds his hands into his eye sockets, says, "Anna, can we talk?"

I stare back at him. "Does . . . Vanessa know you're here?"

Palmer looks at me strangely. "There's nothing going on with me and Vanessa, Anna. Figured you knew me better than that."

"I don't know *what* I know anymore."

It comes out more harshly than I intend. When I see the look in his eyes, I plop down on my bed and open my palm for him to sit with me. We may have ended on mysterious terms, but it doesn't erase the fact that for a couple of months, we were almost inseparable. He literally became my only friend.

"*Okay,*" I say finally.

"You must be pissed, Anna," he says, still standing. "And confused by me, and you probably basically can't stand the sight of my stupid face. And I get why. You should be. But"—turning his palms up helplessly—"I didn't know where else to go. You're the only person I can talk to. The only person who knows me all the way. About my . . . anxiety. Or whatever you wanna call it."

Palmer lowers himself next to me on the bed. At the last second, though, he moves down to the foot—neutral territory. He's quiet for so long, the silence turns into something you can almost hear. Finally he says, "Obviously you've heard . . . the rumors. About me and Wallace and Dylan juicing?"

I nod slowly.

"Well, they're not true."

"Okay."

"They're not true . . . about Dylan and Wallace, anyway."

After another long silence, out comes the truth.

The injury happened. Rehab was slow. The season was going by fast. The deluge of calls from college coaches slowed to a stream, then to a trickle. He got scared. He wanted to play college ball. He didn't want to let his team down. And he *really* didn't want to let his dad down. Dylan knew a guy who knew a guy. Palmer knew Dylan would keep his mouth shut. But he had to break up with me because we were getting so close. Too close. I'd have asked questions. I'd have been able to sense the change in his body. The guilt. It terrified him for me—for anyone—to know him that well.

When Palmer finishes, neither of us speaks for a long, long time. Finally he says, "Please say something, Anna. Just tell me you hate me."

"Wow" is all I can manage. Lame. And I *don't* hate him,

of course. Finally he's being honest. Finally I can see in his eyes that he's done hiding.

The real Palmer is in pain.

I touch his arm gently. It feels more like a sisterly move than anything else.

"Have you talked to anyone else about this?" I ask him finally.

He cups my hand tightly and locks eyes with me. "I'm talking to you."

"Yeah, but, like, a therapist?"

We've had this conversation a couple of times. I mean, we actually had it the day we met. And every time Palmer's given me the same answer: *Meades don't do that.*

Only, tonight he says, "Did you see my search? The one on the Knock List?"

I squint, confused. "I didn't know anything of yours was on there."

"Man," he says with a sad smile. "I thought you'd have seen it right away. *Silver Pines anonymous.*"

I resist the overwhelming urge to say, *That was you?*

"You want to go to SP?" I ask him. "Maybe it's a good idea if you're not—"

"Even before all this," he says, "I wasn't exactly . . . okay." Now he lies back on my bed and closes his eyes. "Anyway. Cat's out now. At least now I don't have to worry about everyone finding out what a messed-up person I am. Everyone knows."

"You made a mistake because you were desperate," I say. "You're not a messed-up person. This is just one tiny thing you did. It's not your whole story."

Palmer's eyes are closed now. It feels so sad, seeing him so depleted. I can't help feeling, though, that we're so far away from the people we were when we were dating. Whatever pheromone-based attraction we initially shared, it's not so powerful anymore. It might even be gone. My mind flashes back to the night we almost had sex: candles, Frank Ocean crooning, his open shirt. We started out by sitting on his bed in almost exactly the same positions we are in now.

And now, suddenly, I realize why I said no. Why I wasn't ready with him.

I hear Jethro saying those three words, and suddenly I know—I care about Palmer, and I feel bad for him, but it's Jethro I wish were here.

It's always been Jethro.

Palmer might think I'm the only person he can talk to, who knows him. But *he'll* never know *me* the way Jethro does. I don't know if I ever wanted him to.

I pull my hand back. Palmer opens his eyes. "I know this is so stressful now, but take it one day at a time." I'm quoting Jethro, I realize. "This story isn't over yet. There's so much that can happen, that can change."

Palmer's eyes are staring at something far away that I can't see or understand. Suddenly they snap back to attention. He straightens up. Immediately I sense that he wants to go. Needs to go. That he feels what all boys—all of us— fear most: rejection.

He pushes himself up from the bed and moves to the window. "Thanks, A. Wish me luck on the way down."

"We're on the first floor."

"Oh yeah." He gives a chuckle, but it's a sad one.

"You really *should* talk to someone about all this," I say.

Palmer holds out a fist for a soft bump. It's the oddest way in the world to say goodbye to your recent ex. But it's the best we can do for now.

Seconds later he's gone. I change into my pajamas and shove the thumb drive into my laptop. A couple of clicks on my track pad, and suddenly I'm looking at Jethro's shaky, first-person video of one of Chuck Close's portraits hanging in the National Gallery. Lou Reed's intense, wrinkled, and wise face stares back at me. And suddenly music starts. Jethro not only took the video, he *scored* it too.

"Sweet Jane" rises and falls through the tinny speakers of my laptop.

15

Six-thirty a.m. My eyes shoot open to the sound of my alarm. I'm lying on top of my covers in bed. There's a metallic taste in my mouth. Someone's voice, midsentence, is filling my ears, coming out of my phone.

". . . so we should be getting another one VERY soon."

I groan and roll onto my side. *Timmy Tepper.* I forgot that I'd set my alarm to whatever was playing.

Now I hear a girl's voice. "How many more leaks do you think we'll get today? We've already got thirteen since midnight, and they're every half hour, so by the end of the day . . ."

Is that *Vanessa*? On Timmy's live stream? Leave it to someone as fickle as Vanessa to start cohosting this godforsaken podcast. It's the biggest megaphone at school right now, and she's got the bull by the horn.

"Almost fifty!" Timmy squeals. "Just think about what'll happen!"

Vanessa starts rattling off the names of the thirteen new victims of the leak, and their significant secrets. I sit up and hold my breath, waiting to hear my name . . .

Meanwhile, everyone's secrets are starting to blend together: sex, drugs, eating issues—all the usuals. What Vanessa and Timmy fail to grasp, as they rattle off one kid's secret addiction to his dad's prescription pills and another's cheating with his ex-girlfriend, is that the most damaging leaks aren't the big secrets that are being revealed or the embarrassing things people learn about us. The most damaging leaks are the tiny little paper cuts that'll lead to the death of our friendships.

Like mine, very soon, if these continue.

But when they get to the end of the list, my name still hasn't come.

Twelve of the new leaks are about Instas and others I don't know that well. Kyle Cherski's the only one I'm at all friends with.

"Kyle is actually a decent digital artist," Vanessa says. "My parents collect modern art—so I should know. These drawings of his that were leaked, they actually look a lot like the Prep kids he's representing. Very realistic. I just hope my Instas don't beat the shit out of him for drawing them being brutally murdered in every way possible."

Part of me can't help but laugh.

Timmy continues, "Before we get the next leak, on behalf of this broadcast, Jethro Stephens, I want to thank you for the tremendous work you are doing. Releasing someone's data every half hour makes our reporting here at TTM—Timmy Tepper Media—*so* much easier. It gives us time to go over each new leak. A grateful nation thanks you for your service!"

So now *everyone* thinks it's Jethro? Wow, these people. I guess it shouldn't come as a surprise that Timmy doesn't care about facts, just like Nichols. The situation's like a comic book to them. Everyone needs their hero or their villain.

I check my phone. I texted Jethro about a dozen times last night. Thank-yous for the video and song. Check-ins about where he's going. But there's no response. Not even a word to let me know he's okay. Now I'm worried more than ever.

"Please. Call me," I text again.

I want to hear his voice so badly. Whatever doubts I had after the Torpedo Factory, whatever confusion I had, it all disappeared last night. Jethro is the one I want. When I see him, I'm going to tell him that *next year* doesn't scare me anymore. Or any year. I'm going to tell him that after this mess is over, we can even take a year off school and go to all the places we've dreamed of going.

"As I mentioned earlier," Timmy says now, "Jethro Stephens isn't on Facebook or Twitter or Instagram. I'm just checking a couple of Yik Yak and Whisper threads again right now, Vanessa, for the most up-to-date information. They've been Gamergate hot all night, as you know. Lotta people out there threatening Jethro if he ever shows up at school again. Couple of anonymous posters saying they're gonna bomb his house or whatever school he decides to finish out the year at."

I take my phone with me into the bathroom, set it down on the sink, and splash my face with cold water. It can't possibly be cold enough. I wish I could jump into a frozen lake and never come back up, with what I'm hearing right now.

Vanessa pipes up. "What happened to Haven Dodd was a shame, and even if Jethro Stephens is responsible—as we now believe he *is*—we want to remind you all, we don't condone trolling or SWATing or violence. As my yoga teacher says, *shanti.*"

It's so, so obvious from her tone that what Vanessa is really saying is, *JETHRO STEPHENS did this to you. Do what you will.* I hate her.

Timmy chimes in. "We'll be back to Jethro in a moment, Vanessa—and we will have some updates on that very question, in point of fact. In the meantime, drumroll . . . YES! We have another leak at the newest posting site Jethro Stephens is using, Prepforhell.com!"

A terrible feeling creeps into my stomach. Nausea.

I know it's going to be me.

Timmy whistles loudly. "And the six-thirty leak appears to be . . . oh my . . . the editor of propaganda at the *Xandria*. RADHIKA MEHTA, everyone! Check. It. Out!"

I immediately stand from the toilet, hit Stop on Timmy's live stream, and run back into my bedroom. I turn my phone OFF. Toss it on the bed facedown.

No, I will not listen to Timmy and Vanessa dissect Rad's inner life.

No, I will not look at the website.

No, I will not judge my friend.

Should I call Rad right now and make sure she's okay?

I need a moment to process. I jump in the shower and let the hot water run over my face, my eyes, my hair. I scrub and scrub and condition and stretch and do anything else to avoid getting out. It's the longest shower I've ever taken.

Twenty minutes later I'm a prune. I get dressed and finally pick up my phone.

There's not a word from Rad.

But I have more than thirty texts from Nikki.

"She told me she was sorry for Mattie a thousand times!" Nikki screams at me. "And when she was apologizing, she forgot to mention she's a big, fat fucking liar."

I'm sitting in Nikki's bedroom as she rifles through her closet, pulling shoes and clothes out and tossing them onto the Anthropologie coverlet beside me.

Nikki continues, "Rad is the girl in that Kevin Spacey movie she made us watch last year—the fake deep one with the stupid plastic bag blowing in the wind. I *hated* that movie. What's it called?" She stops throwing stuff on the bed and gives me an impatient exhalation when I don't answer right away.

"*American Beauty?*" I finally offer, racking my brain.

"Yes! She's what's-her-name's character."

"Mena Suvari's?"

"Did Mena Sue Whatever play the dumb skeeze who's actually an even dumber virgin, so dumb she tries to get Kevin Spacey, who's clearly gay, to have sex with her?"

Nikki turns back into the closet.

"Kevin Spacey might be gay in real life," I say, "but I don't think his character in that movie was supposed to be—" Then I interrupt myself, realizing that isn't Nikki's point. Finally I say, "Yes, that's the character Mena Suvari plays."

Nikki turns and raises her voice, even louder now. "Then that's who Rad is. God, I could kill her! She ruined my life. You know what she did? She *reverse* slut-shamed me."

Basically, Rad's big reveal was . . . well, how *little* there is to reveal.

Yeah, Rad visited the website of a local plastic surgeon. She also bought the photo app Pixtr, which gives you an instant nose job. But those are the only two leaks of hers that are in any way titillating or salacious. Other than that, zippo. There were no sexts or dirty-talk chats or thong self-ies. All her messages and photos were PG-13, even the ones she sent to Andrew, who I know she'd hooked up with. In fact, if it weren't for the many F-bombs she dropped, the messages would be strictly PG, forget the 13. And what about all the older guys she's busy spurning high school guys for? Those oh-so experienced men with advanced sexual techniques and superior game? Unless Rad was communicating with them via Bat Signal, they don't exist.

Rad's double life is, apparently, also an *imaginary* life.

I'm not exactly mad at her. Overall, the texts and DMs she sent to Nikki about me while I was with Palmer are a little harsh, but she didn't say anything to Nikki she wouldn't have said to my face. *Anna has a stick of butter for a spine. She's supposed to be some rebel artist? Georgia O'Keeffe would be so proud (sarcastic voice).*

"I never would have hooked up with Mattie if it weren't for her baiting me," Nikki's saying now. "And even if I did, I never would have had sex with him. You know Rad told me you should always give boys a five-minute blow job before sex? That it's, like, a requirement? All of it. All the comments, RedTube, all the assholes who call me Two of Clubs now . . . none of it would have happened if Rad hadn't lied."

I want to remind her that the person to blame here for RedTube and "Two of Clubs" is Mattie Eizenberg, but what Nikki wants to do now is vent. She drags something from the back of her closet. One of those red Container Store letterboxes with rough felt on the outside. She rips off the lid and starts dumping the contents into her trash bin.

It's her Rad memory box, I realize as birthday cards and tickets to shows at Wolf Trap and other keepsakes flutter into the garbage. Nikki has one for me in the back of her closet too, I know. Some girls keep boxes like these so they can remember every detail of some floppy-haired boy they once loved. Or still do. But instead of boy stuff, Nikki's been keeping souvenirs of our decade-long friendships in her red boxes.

"I don't think she *meant* to hurt you, Nik."

Nikki looks at me. There's rage in her eyes. "I know, with everything happening with Jethro and Haven now, it must seem like I'm making a huge deal out of this, A. But it *is* a big deal. I trusted Rad. I thought I knew her. It's not even the deck of cards, or the sex, or any of that. That I can take. What I can't take is that I told Rad every secret I have, every insecurity, totally truthfully, for years. And she lied about everything. I don't even have any idea who I've been friends with all this time. She's a psychopath."

Nikki takes a long breath and puts her head on my shoulder. "I'm sorry things ever got bad between *us*. Now I know you're the only person I can really trust."

As I push through the early-morning crowd and approach my locker, I find Rad sitting in front of it, legs sprawled out wide like a cowboy's, her classic thinking pose.

"Did you get my messages?" I ask her when we have some privacy.

"Yes," she says, standing. "Do you know if Nikki got mine?"

"Rad . . ."

"I left ten. No. Eleven."

"You gotta understand how's she feeling right now. . . ."

Rad bangs her head softly against the metal of my locker. "This wasn't some grand plan!" she says. "It started as the smallest freaking possible fib! In seventh grade I told you guys I got felt up at camp by this guy I had a crush on who was two years older and didn't know I existed, never

186

even looked at me. I didn't want you to think nothing happened to me all summer. And then things snowballed. I woke up one day and my entire identity was an actual version of Emma Stone in *Easy A*."

"But I mean, you really laid it on heavy with Nik."

"The story became real *for me*," Rad says. "I played the part. And, Nikki—God. I thought it was what she wanted. She asked me for help, so I *told* her how I played the part. I didn't know the Hackergate extravaganza would descend on Prep. And obviously I didn't know that Mattie would turn out to be such a scumbag."

"Just give Nikki space," I say. "Time too."

"So I guess now it's just liar me and abandoner you. Guess I've descended to your level." But her voice is meek. Finally she drops the bravado and says, "Think Nikki will ever forgive me? I mean, she forgave you, right?"

"I guess so. Yeah."

Rad pushes my shoulder. "Well, you should count your lucky stars."

"Why?"

"That you're a boring texter. Or you might not be going to RISD after all."

She's right. Rad and I must have sent each other more than ten thousand texts in the last five years, since we got our phones. But we saved our bitchiest talk for in person.

If only I'd been more boring when I was texting Palmer.

After a long silence, Rad whispers, "Anything from Jethro?"

I shake my head.

"Haven's back," she says. "Totally messed up about the

Jethro thing. I think Haven might murder his dad." Rad stares off down the hallway. "Maybe I should find him. Ask him to put me out of my misery instead."

A mixture of acrylic, turpentine, clay, patchouli, and oddly inoffensive body odor is in the air as I walk inside the art lab. Mr. Touhey's old-fashioned, paint-spattered stereo is playing a Jefferson Airplane CD. At least one person is refusing to be cowed or changed by the leaks.

"Anna. Welcome to the party," he says.

I stare, confused. Party? He points toward the back of the room. A bunch of students are clustered around Kyle Cherski's workstation. They're laughing and pointing at his drawings with *awe*. No one is beating Kyle up. No, Mr. Too Marginal to Even Be on the Periphery is now the center of attention, apparently all thanks to the leak and the legion of new fans of his Instagram-bashing caricatures.

I do my best to block out the sounds of Kyle's fans and focus on my self-portrait. Settling into my work space, I stare at the light-pink contours of my own lips, my too-square-for-a-girl jawline. I take a brush and try to add some shadow on my chin, but I'm rearranging deck chairs on the *Titanic*.

My brush goes down. I close my eyes.

When I started this piece, it all made sense to me. I wanted a self-portrait that represented the central duality of my life: how I see myself versus how others see me. But now—after everything that's happened—I'm not sure it's

"And you have absolutely *no* idea where he might be?"

"Hiding from the PTA and their pitchforks?" I laugh nervously.

"This is a serious matter, Ms. Soler."

"Falsely accusing my friend of hurting all of us without any proof? Or the school app illegally recording all our data in the first place?"

Luckily, miraculously, I don't cross whatever line would have gotten me into trouble with Headmaster Nichols today. I'm excused from the administration office after giving a promise to let them know if I find out anything about where he is.

Yeah, right.

I slump out of the office and head to lunch.

Nikki made me promise I'd sit with her, and I'm keeping my word despite the fact that a crowded dining hall is the last hell on earth I want to be in right now. There's no wait at the salad bar, so I grab a tray, throw a couple of lettuce leaves on a plate, a few tomatoes and tofu chunks, then pour on blue-cheese dressing. I'm a huge eater, normally. Like, *chocolate is terrified when it hears my footsteps* huge.

I get a fork and a napkin and begin the long walk to the seating area through a cacophony of noise and arguments and gossip, half the room secretly looking at their phones. I watch a girl I don't know dump a plate of food in a senior boy's lap as he calls her a whore. Here's a sophomore yelling at her friends about her supposed Oxy addiction and storming off. There's a junior cackling and showing dirty selfies from one of the leaks to guys I barely know. *Ashes, ashes, we all fall down.*

How benign this place used to be—how ordered and controlled and quaint. How could it ever have scared me? Every group had its own table and section of the room. Each group might not have respected or liked every other group, but at least all the groups recognized one another's right to physically exist and breathe Prep air.

Now the vibe is animalistic. In fact, I have a new understanding of the expression *dog eat dog*. The kids in this room seem to have gone in one of two directions, both canine: junkyard dog, frothing at the mouth, ready to rip out a throat; or abused rescue, cringing in the corner.

I spot Nikki.

She's at a table in the back with Andrew. Like practically everyone else, they're buried in their phones. Teachers aren't bothering to even try to enforce the no-cell-phone rule anymore. They probably don't have the energy to put up a fight.

As I sit with them, I see Rad ten feet away, holding her tray uncertainly. And I can tell from the angle of her head that she's watching Nikki. Finally she takes a small step forward.

Nikki looks up from her iPhone. She places it on the table and slams her hands down to cover the chair Rad is hovering over. Like, *physically* blocks her from sitting down. "Do me a favor, Rad. Get out of my sight."

Rad's blinking rapidly, trying to keep the tears away.

Andrew intervenes. "Don't be such a hard-ass, Nik. We're all still friends here."

Nikki, looking at Andrew but chucking a thumb in Rad's direction, says, "*She* is not my friend. Friends don't lie to friends about who they are." I feel my stomach go watery as Nikki continues: "And, Andrew, you might be feeling all warm and fuzzy and special right now because Rad let you touch her tits or whatever, and it looks like you're the only guy who's ever done that, but spare me, okay?"

Rad starts to say something. "Nik—"

But she's cut off by the sound of Timmy Tepper's voice: "Tepper here with Vanessa Eubanks to give you dish with your lunch." His voice leaps out of Nikki's cell phone speaker and the cell phone speakers of practically everyone else in the dining hall. Nikki stares at her phone, refusing to look at Rad.

Rad wipes the tears on her face and hurries away. It's the first time I've seen her cry in years. I want to follow her, to drape my arm over her shoulder and remind her to breathe. I start to stand. But as I do, Nikki turns to me, anger in her eyes. An edge in her voice I'm not used to. "So, Anna. Who are you eating lunch with today?"

I drop back into my seat. This is a lose-lose situation.

That's when I hear Vanessa's voice coming through Nikki's phone. "The saddest thing is that Palmer didn't even sign yet. Maybe if he'd committed earlier they could sweep it under the rug. But what school in their right mind would want to sign him now?"

Then Timmy: "The steroids might not even show up in his system anymore."

"Doesn't matter," Vanessa says cheerfully. "He's damaged goods."

"Can you, like, turn that off, please?" I snap. Nikki looks

surprised. "Look," I tell her, "I'm sorry, but I can't take it anymore. First Jethro, now Palmer? No one deserves to be strung up like this, not even the dude who dumped me."

Nikki leans in. "Have you talked to him?"

I sigh. "Yes. Whatever Palmer and I were before . . . he's still my friend, and he's in pain. And Vanessa has gotten away with too much of this shit."

It's then that I realize—against all my SAD instincts—I have to go talk to Vanessa.

It's time to stop her.

I go to the senior lounge. And wait. Half an hour later Vanessa finally struts past, returning from whatever secret location she and Timmy are recording the live stream from off campus, and I quietly follow her to the first-floor bathroom. She doesn't seem to see me, or she's just completely ignoring me. She's applying liquid eyeliner as I walk into one of the stalls and find a plunger, then walk back out and jam the wooden end tightly between the door bottom and the floor so no one can come in.

I know she knew I was here, but it takes *this* to get her to look at me.

"Here's the deal," I begin. "There's a lot of messed-up stuff going around these days. The last thing Palmer needs right now is you out there saying crap about him," I tell her. "Any chance he has to figure this out, you're making it worse for him."

Vanessa glances back at me in the mirror. "Don't worry, it can't get any worse. They're saying he brought the drugs to school now. Like, kept them in his locker, so he might not even be able to graduate. You should just be glad I decided to leave that part out."

"I thought you were his friend," I say, shaking my head in disbelief. "Are you mad 'cause he doesn't want you? Or are you just throwing Palmer under the bus so you can make everyone forget what *you* are?"

Vanessa works on her mascara. "Yeah? What's that?"

"An attention whore? A cheerleader who thinks it matters? Or . . . how about a vulture, eating whatever piece of Instagram boy meat is freshest? How long did it take after we were done before you were all over Palmer?"

Finally Vanessa turns directly to me. "I think you're still a little drunk on your fifteen minutes, Anna. Don't worry, the hangover's coming."

"Just stop talking about him, Vanessa."

"I'm pretty sure *you* should be talking about him and everything else," she says. Now Vanessa crosses her arms and smiles. "To your therapist, that is. Maybe she can tell you how to *avoid rebounding with a close friend*."

"What?"

"Or how about *how to fix a friend breakup*? Why don't you start with not ditching all *your* friends?"

I've never gotten physically violent in my life. But right now Vanessa stares at me with a disgusted little smirk, and I want to punch her right in her overly whitened teeth. Shatter them *Insurgent* virtual reality–style.

"The worst part is," Vanessa continues, "you think you and Palmer were *actually* boyfriend and girlfriend. It was so sad, really."

Some defense mechanism goes off in my brain, and I can't resist saying, "Really, Vanessa? 'Cause Palmer was at my house last night, trying to get back together with me."

"I'm not talking about Palmer."

I squint at her. "Think you might be the drunk one, Vanessa."

Vanessa reaches back into her purse, pulls out a tube of lip gloss. "*You* were the one faking it. You ditched the people you belong with because you wanted Palmer to convince everyone else that you aren't the freak you know you are inside. That's what *all* you people do. You're so desperate for one of us to smile at you! Then we do, and you forget about the fact that you never liked basketball or drinking at parties or any of the rest of it. You try to become someone else—someone people might mistake for interesting. And *that's* why you sayonara'd your friends, Anna. Not because Palmer needed you to. You got rid of them because it's a lot harder to sell yourself a lie about who you really are when people who've known you for years are still hanging around."

"You've been a delusional bitch since sixth grade," I spit. "No one cared about you before middle school, and no one will care about you after we leave high school."

I slap the lip gloss from her hand.

Except I don't.

My hand totally whiffs, and the momentum of my arm sends me in a quarter circle. I'm so dizzy that I just slapped the air.

"Wow, Soler," Vanessa says, applying her lip gloss calmly. "Just . . . wow."

I turn, remove the plunger from under the door, and throw it across the bathroom. I'm shaking from head to toe as I walk out of Ewing and onto the quad. It's an unusually warm day. I think I hear birds chirping, but I'm in such a daze, I really can't focus on what's happening around me. I don't know where I'm going, so eventually I stop. In front of me is Dwight Library. A couple of sophomore girls play Hacky Sack nearby.

As I try to regain my balance, a buzzer pierces my eardrums.

The school PA rings out across the quad. Nichols's voice booms through it.

"Lunch is cut short. All students report to the nearest classroom, administrative office, or gymnasium immediately. We are on a schoolwide lockdown, and no one is coming in or out. This is not a drill."

16

OUT THE LIBRARY WINDOWS, WE SEE TWO ALEXANDRIA POLICE patrol cars swerve off the street and onto campus. They come to a quick stop in front of the main administration building. Four cops hop out, and a female officer brings out a huge German shepherd from the backseat. If this were a drill, of which there are two each year, then these officers would not be in a rush. Already the hashtag #*Prep-Lockdown* is blowing up. I scan through Snapchat and see phrases like *weapons threat called in* and *maniac on the loose.*

As far as I know, this is the first time police have ever been on campus for something real. I'm still feeling dizzy.

Out of the corner of my eye, I see an arm waving furiously at me. It belongs to Haven, sitting at a table catty-corner from mine. I haven't seen him since last night, before the Prep parents' meeting. It's the first time he's been back at school this week. I walk over, relieved to see a friendly face, and kneel next to him.

"You okay?" I ask as he pulls out his earbuds.

"I mean, kinda. But I'm not the one to worry about."

"Nothing from Jethro?"

He shakes his head somberly.

A librarian appears at my side—apparently I've overstepped the lockdown rules for a hair too long, and I'm escorted back to my seat. Haven rolls his eyes behind the librarian's back and, waving bye to me, puts his earbuds back in. Others around the room are pulling headphones on too, I notice, and I know why.

A sophomore at the table behind mine is playing the live stream at a really low volume. As much as I want to say, *Can you turn that garbage off?* I sit still, listening.

". . . Nichols got me on a technicality. That's right, loyal listeners, suspended for one week, as of two minutes ago. You heard it here first." Timmy sounds a little wounded. "What's interesting is that a lot of student behavior—much of it covered in depth by this podcast—is grounds for a suspension, but none of those students have been punished by the Prep administration. Does anyone else smell a witch hunt? Well, I won't be intimidated or bullied into silence."

A few kids pump their fists in the air in support.

"There is a lot to cover today," Timmy says, off and running, "including up-to-the-minute updates on the NCAA investigation into Palmer Meade's steroid use. Apparently he is now being forced to submit to testing by every university interested in him. And the drugs he juiced with can stay in your system for up to forty days. Time to do some calendar math, people."

As I focus on breathing calmly in my chair, I imagine throwing the iPad out the glass window, smashing that little weasel's voice to bits.

"But before we get to that and other pressing items, we have a listener request. Radhika Mehta, pseudo sexual sophisticate and editor in chief of the *Xandria*, just sent an unusual one in."

Huh?

Timmy clears his throat, then plays a drumroll sound effect. *"Dear Nikki, Most of the people who've been exposed at Prep deserved it, one way or another. Let's face it. But you are a genuinely nice person. Without a mean bone in your body."*

Timmy pauses, as if to let that sink in, then keeps going. *"I want your trust back. The first step is this open letter to tell you and the whole school how badly I treated you and to beg for your forgiveness. You already know it, but so does everyone else now: I am a fake (like a lot of the other schmucks at Alexandria Prep), and, worse than that, I goaded you and lied to your face. But I love you, Nik. I wish I could take it all back, and I wish you could find a way to love me back again, despite the idiotic things I've done. Love, your hopefully bestie one day again, Radhika."*

Oh God. No. What was Rad thinking?

It's the most earnest thing Rad has ever said in her life. She's obviously just so, so desperate. But using Timmy as her voice?

I look over and see Haven with his face in his palm.

"Now that was an honest, if slightly syrupy, gesture, I think we'll all agree," Timmy says. "There is a teachable moment to be—" But Timmy stops. "Hang on—in just this second, it looks like we may have *a response* already! From Nikki Davis, whose story you're all perhaps a *little too* familiar with!"

I cringe.

"*Fuck you*," it begins, "*you fucking bitch.*" Timmy pauses now. "Actually, people, that appears to be all of it."

The thought then crosses my mind . . . I bet Timmy's the one who called in the threat, to retaliate for his suspension! Or to give himself a captive audience.

He continues with the conviction of the reborn. "What we're seeing is that a strong dose of the truth is what we all need," Timmy says. "Which is a perfect segue to my next guest. Aiden 'Mac' McDonald. Mac's account on the gay hookup site Grindr was leaked in the last round. That he has an account was, of course, news to his girlfriend, Alexis Bowman. But today, Mac has decided that, although painful, sunshine is sometimes the best disinfectant. So he's agreed to tell us the names of some of the other gays longing to be free."

"This isn't funny," Mac says, joining in. "But I've come to think it's *important*."

Holy crap. Are they doing what I think they're doing?

"Sounds like you're ready to throw open those closet doors."

Suddenly, as if on cue, the doors of the library fly open. In come the police with their simultaneously adorable yet terrifying canine team, who do a quick sweep of the library. And on Timmy's show, out the names get dragged.

This is intense, to say the least.

Sandy Gillis, a sophomore on the football team.

Geoff Ames, a junior on the baseball team.

Last but not least: *Andrew Yang, a senior on the lacrosse team.*

'Scuse me?

Haven is furrowing his brow and staring at me.

"Andrew?" I text him from across the room.

Haven texts back:

Don't know what to think anymore. I could be gay. You could be a dude. Which would be fine. But, just saying, nothing would surprise me anymore.

Andrew has always been a solo-YOLO-type guy. Avoids proms. Avoids dates. Avoids girls except for Rad . . . who he was *supposedly* sleeping with. Oh man, now I see: they *used* each other. Not as sex toys. As—what do you call it?—*beards.*

I don't care about the fact that Andrew's gay—of course not; it's the twenty-teens, get over it. But it makes me pretty sad for Andrew that he thought he had to keep it a secret from all of us now that the secret's out there.

I slam my eyes shut like a little kid trying to make everything disappear.

Now Nichols is back on the speaker system.

The sweep came up with nothing.

The lockdown is over.

We find Andrew kicking the chain-link fence with the toe of his Converse. Good to know the more things change, the more he still wants to smoke weed in the same place. "Hey, dudes," he says when he sees us.

I feel my throat constrict when I see how bloodshot his eyes are. He's been smoking, I'm sure, but I think he's also been crying. I step forward and give him a quick hug. I breathe easier when he returns the embrace.

After a few seconds, he gently pulls away and looks at us sadly. "It's been a shit day, you know? I'm sorry I wasn't the one to tell you guys. I wanted to, but it didn't feel right to before I told my mom and dad, and there's no way I was going to tell them. So . . ." He trails off. For several seconds he's quiet, concentrating. Then he goes on, "I'm going to have to tell them now, though. Tonight, at the latest. If I don't, they'll either get it from the Net, or some friend of my mom's will give her the news that her son's a fag."

I wince when he uses that word. I can feel Haven beside me wince too.

"Please don't talk like that, Andrew," Haven says. "Nobody cares that you're gay. At least, nobody who really matters."

Andrew lets out a joyless laugh. "Except my parents."

"We could go with you when you tell them. Safety in numbers?"

Andrew shakes his head. "Thanks, but I've got to do this one alone. I mean, everybody's got their own shit to deal with these days. Me, Nikki, now Jethro."

"You heard from him?" I squeal.

"Twenty minutes ago."

My heart feels like it's going to thump out of my chest. "Jesus, what did he say?"

Andrew shrugs. "It was from a random number, probably a burner. Said he's so sorry this is happening to me. To stay strong. I texted back, saying I know he didn't do the leaks, that we could fight what people are saying about him."

"Did he respond?" I ask.

Andrew looks down, then up again. "The crazy thing is, he said he's leaving in twenty-four hours. Probably never coming back."

"C'mon," Haven says, laughing darkly. "That seems a little dramatic. I mean, where's he gonna go?"

"He said everyone thinks he's responsible. That he's got no other choice."

My heart starts to race. I turn to Haven. "We have to find him."

Haven says to Andrew, "Dude, can you give me that burner number?"

Once Andrew does, Haven gives him a hug. Not a weak man hug. A real hug—full contact, full body. A hug that delivers the message that he loves Andrew no matter what. I kiss Andrew's cheek and squeeze his hand. He gives a smile and then crouches down, packing another bowl.

"What are you gonna do?" Haven asks. "Do you want to come with us?"

Andrew shakes his head. "I need to smoke this, then I

need to tell my parents. Course, I *was* thinking about beating the shit out of someone on the way home."

Haven sniffs. "Who? Mac? For outing you?"

"Nah," Andrew says. "I was thinking Mattie Eizenberg. He has it coming, right? Plus, it just feels like a good story to tell my kids someday. Like, rather than the gay Asian dude getting beat up after being pushed out of the closet, he goes and lays a serious beat-down on some straight misogynist dude who messed with *his* friends."

My head is swirling. "Better in theory than in reality, probably. Don't do anything you'll regret," I tell him. "Please."

"Good luck finding J," he tells us, returning to his bowl. "And thanks."

17

Jethro lives with his mom in Columbia Heights, on a street that's somewhere between okay and iffy. Their rental house is small and strangely bald-looking—there are no trees or bushes around it, and the front yard is more dirt than grass.

Today his dead-end block looks even spookier than usual. The house is tagged from top to bottom. Words varying from *hacker* to *fag* to *troll* are graffitied across the door, the brick of the house, even the small, dilapidated porch. The lidless eyes of the windows have spiderwebs or are shattered entirely. The swing Jethro and I have sat on a thousand times—where we've debated everything from our favorite Grimes song to the worst Tarantino movie—is on the ground, the chain cut.

We walk to the front, stepping over the overturned and

broken outdoor furniture. "This is all my *dad's* fault," Haven says, surveying the damage. "What a dick."

Jethro hasn't returned any of our texts on the burner number Andrew gave us. And Haven and I both know: Jethro's one of the smartest people we know. If he doesn't want to be found, he won't be found. Not even by us.

I press my face to the glass of one of the windows. The living room has an enormous television, a PlayStation, and two leather recliners, but also a dining table with a lilac tablecloth, packed bookshelves, and some cheery floral wallpaper. Decor that is a compromise between a mother and her son. Given what it looks like out here, it's kind of surprising that the living room looks exactly as I remember it.

Haven's eyes open wide, as if he just remembered something.

He hurries to the edge of the yard and crouches down beside a small cast-iron turtle, then slides off the turtle's shell and pulls out a key.

I haven't been in Jethro's bedroom since pre-Palmer times. Which is weird, since he and I have had sex in the meantime. It smells more like Jethro in here than even he does—a kind of magnified version of his soap and aftershave and something unnameable that makes my heart ache ever so slightly. The bed is messy; the shades are down. On the walls hanging in front of Haven and me: a poster for *Mr. Robot* in Chinese, Sleater-Kinney and Deerhunter vinyls slapped up with grip tape.

"Maybe he went to his gram's in New York," Haven says.

"I already tried calling her," I say. "Unless she's the best eighty-year-old liar in the world, she hasn't seen Jethro since last Easter."

Now Haven holds up Jethro's copy of Neal Stephenson's *Snow Crash*. "Cal Tech would probably still take him even if they thought he did this. MIT might not, but Cal Tech is more . . . forgiving. Maybe he finally manifested his destiny."

"Jethro said if he ever went to California, he'd take me with him." I swallow the tiny knot in my throat.

Haven shrugs. "You really think he'll just leave?"

"Wouldn't you?" I ask, sifting through the papers Jethro's left on his desk, searching for any clue about where he might have gone. An address, a number, anything.

I freeze in place when I catch a glimpse of something sitting where his computer normally goes (it's not here, of course, but this is the one clean area of the desk). On a small canvas is a half-finished oil painting of a Steinway piano turned inside out, strings popped and keys strewn across a jazz-club floor.

I blink. I know that painting well. I hated it so much that I threw it away even after it had crossed the Rubicon—the point of no return—that Mr. Touhey always talks about. You have to finish what you've started once you've invested more than forty hours in it—that's his rule. A week's work. But in this case, I ignored Touhey's rule. Jethro probably rescued it from the trash. That must have been a year ago, at least. Maybe he thought I would change my mind someday. That I would finish it for him.

"I could DM some of his camp friends," Haven says. "See if they've heard anything. I think I might follow a couple of them on Instagram."

"Why not," I tell him. Haven pulls out his phone, starts typing and swiping furiously. I can't look at my piano anymore, so I plop down on the bed, take in the room one last time. Up until a few months ago, this room was like a home away from home. How many times have I sat right here, listening to Jethro tell me about the virtues of slasher films, or the importance of goats to people in developing countries, or all the reasons why applied math is better than theoretical?

Applied math.

Something clicks in my mind. In one corner of Jethro's room, all his awards and trophies have been stuffed and piled up. But in Jethro's case they aren't track medals or soccer trophies. They're from science fairs and Odyssey of the Mind and *It's Academic.* I hop back up from the bed and start looking through them. There's one in particular I want to find. I've seen it once or twice, when the sun hit the little pyramid at just the right angle.

"This is from that nerd Super Bowl you two were part of, right?" I ask Haven once I've got it in my sweaty palm.

"Nerd Super Bowl?" Haven shakes his head in disbelief. "*Mathletes,* Anna. The math olympiad. Only the most competitive calculus prize on this side of the Atlantic—"

"Yeah, yeah, sorry," I say, studying the plaque at the

bottom. "Look, weren't there a couple of seniors on the team with you? Other hackers?"

"Garrett and Peter? I called them, looking for J, already."

WINNERS: GARRETT KEATING, PETER CERVIERI,
JETHRO STEPHENS, HAVEN DODD

"What did they say?"

"That they hadn't heard from him."

"Where are they?"

"College," Haven says. "Well, Peter's already in a master's program, actually, after only two years. They're both at Johns Hopkins."

Johns Hopkins? Didn't Jethro say he was in touch with someone there?

Palming my keys, I move out into the hall. "What's the prize for finding missing friends wanted by the police?"

According to the GPS on Haven's phone, the drive was supposed to take us only an hour and fifteen minutes, but it takes us that long just to get up the Baltimore–Washington Parkway and into Baltimore. Jethro and I binge-watched *The Wire* over July Fourth weekend, and it's the first time I've seen D.C.'s sister/rival city since. Jethro and Haven's friends share an off-campus apartment near Johns Hopkins, and finally we make it to their neighborhood. Just row after row of brick townhouses. I wonder if this is what I should expect on the RISD campus.

Haven presses the buzzer for, like, a minute. "These

guys are nocturnal," he says. "We need to get them out of their coffins."

"It's five p.m.," I say, wrinkling my nose.

"Exactly."

After another minute, there's the sound of feet clomping down steps, and then an irritated male voice saying, "Jesus, wait a second, wait a second. I'm coming!"

I'm starting to feel the nerves that automatically crash down on me when I'm about to meet someone new. Next thing I know, the door's thrown open by a tall, slightly overweight guy with thick, blue glasses, in a *Shrek* T-shirt. Headphones are dangling around his neck, heavy metal blasting out of them. Not too intimidating, anyhow.

"G Moneypenny," Haven says.

"Haven!" Blue Glasses says with a grin.

"Garrett, this is Anna," Haven says.

Garrett looks at me for a second, as if he's trying to place my face. "Come on in. And sorry for the hostile greeting. I thought Pete had forgotten his keys again."

He leads us through a dark hallway into a kitchen area. It's somewhere between boy dirty and boy filthy, the sink piled high with dishes, the microwave door thrown open, the insides splattered red, flies buzzing around a spot of what looks like dried maple syrup on the counter. In one corner is a life-size statue of Daisy Ridley as her *Star Wars* character, toting a badass fighting staff. On the fridge is a magnet that says THERE'S NO PLACE LIKE 127.0.0.1.

Garrett tugs the refrigerator handle and then sticks his head inside. "Want OJ that may or may not have expired? Grape Crush that's definitely gone flat?"

"Um, Garrett," I say awkwardly, dropping a paper-towel square on the seat of a chair before sitting on it, "we're actually here to find Jethro."

Garrett stares into the fridge without looking back. "Jethro? I told Haven here we haven't heard from him. Sorry. But tell J we said hey if you do."

"You haven't heard from him?"

"Nope."

I give Haven a look, but he just shrugs.

I'm not giving up. Not on Jethro. Deep breath, then: "So, Jethro told me that he was gonna get you guys to help him find out who hacked our school's system. That you guys were figuring out some algorithm or whatever."

"That's not what an algorithm is."

"*O-kay*, can you not mansplain to me what an algorithm is? We're here to find Jethro. *That's* what's important right now."

"Just told you," Garrett says. "No idea where he is." He closes the fridge and turns to Haven. "Can you hit her Off switch, dude?"

I feel heated, like my face is flushed. I'm pissed. And sick of beating around the bush in this nerd bro's gross kitchen. "You must know what's going on at Prep, right?"

Looking uncomfortable, he squares the THERE'S NO PLACE LIKE 127.0.0.1 magnet with his thumb. "Yeah, we saw. Who hasn't?"

"Then you know everyone thinks Jethro's behind the leaks, right?" I say. "They think he intentionally posted our friends' and everyone else's stuff, despite the fact that he would never do anything *remotely* like that. Now he's gonna run, and everyone who thinks he did it will have all the proof they need. He'll lose everything he's worked for. He'll lose his place at MIT." I'm pacing around the middle of the kitchen now, practically panting. I feel my eyes get wet just from saying those words out loud. "So if you have any idea where he is, maybe you should be a real friend to him and tell us so we can get him to put an end to all this."

Garrett glances over at Haven. "Like I said, would love to help. Unfortunately, Jethro hasn't been here in months, and I have some coding to get to. Maybe while I'm at it, I'll build, like, a really cool algorithm."

Haven looks at him seriously. "Garrett, c'mon, we're trying to help Jethro."

"Look, dude," he says, nodding toward the front door. "Nothing else to see here. Wish there was something else I could do."

Droopy-shouldered and defeated, Haven and I make our way back to the car.

I drop into the driver's seat, and my head sags onto the steering wheel. The leather feels cool against my forehead.

I can't really think of where to go next. Jethro has a much older half sister in Chicago, but they're not close. Could he have gone *there* already?

I feel so helpless.

"Yo," I hear Haven say. He points through the windshield.

And there stands Jethro in the doorway to the apartment. He must have been hiding from us somewhere in the back. Now he's on the porch.

"What!" I shriek. "Is he kidding?"

I jump out of the car and run to him. After this wild-goose chase of a day, I almost expect him to run when he sees us. But he's still. His eyes are red, and he looks exhausted. I fling my arms around him.

I pull away from our embrace so I can see his face. "Tell me you're okay," I say.

"I'm okay."

"We were so worried. God, I was so worried!" I'm rambling now, words piling out. "Please, come home with us. We'll get it all figured out, I promise."

Jethro sighs and tips his head back. "There's nothing to figure out, Anna."

"Of course there is. We'll prove you had nothing to do with this."

"That's the problem," Jethro says. "I did."

We sit on the hard cement stoop in silence. I have a million questions, but I'm going to let him do the talking. Haven went back inside with Garrett after Jethro asked him to give us a few minutes in private. Jethro pulls out a cigarette he must have gotten from Garrett or Pete—I've never seen him smoke before. He cups his hand and protects the flame of his lighter against the wind coming in off the harbor, then takes a long drag.

"A couple days after Christmas," he says finally, "I was at Wiseguy Pizza, picking up a pie for me and mom. Palmer and Wallace walk in the door and get in line behind me. I had my hood up, and I guess Palmer didn't see me standing there. Anyway, I heard Palmer telling Wallace that you and he were done."

I have no idea why, but something about the way this story is starting makes me run cold. I cross my arms across my chest. Once upon a time Jethro would have wrapped an arm around me. Not today.

"So," he says finally. "The Torpedo Factory was what— less than a week later? And, like I told you, Anna, it was the best night of my life."

"I'm sorry," I say. "I know I—"

"Wait," he interrupts, his voice a little harsh. "Don't say you're sorry to me. You can't do that. That's not what this is. And I don't deserve it." He takes another drag off the cigarette. "Anyway. After you and I talked the next day . . . my head wasn't on straight. When you told me you might still be in love with him, I lost my shit."

I stare at him, in shock, barely able to process the words.

Jethro continues. "That night I was staring at the leaked search terms. Probably trying to figure out which ones were his. I don't know. But I realized something, and I went dig- ging. If search terms were being recorded by the app, I thought maybe *everything* was being recorded. *Including* anything Palmer wrote to you or anyone else on his phone. At first it was just my morbid curiosity. I had to see if you guys were talking again. If he wanted you back too. Or if he was being enough of a dick to you that you'd change your mind."

My body feels frozen. Jethro takes one more puff on the cigarette and then puts it out. I try to keep my breath steady and not to look away from the spot in the concrete that my eyes have arbitrarily fixated on. If I do, I might spiral somewhere I don't want to go. A couple of what I assume are Johns Hopkins sorority girls walk by, laughing and blowing out cold winter air. They look happy, and right now I wish I were going wherever they are—headed off to get loaded at a sorority party or to watch foreign movies or whatever college kids here do.

"It's sad how easy it was to get access," Jethro continues. "A little code plus some social engineering on the network admins, and I saw everything that the Prep for Today app recorded from our phones. An hour later I could see everything anyone had written about Palmer, and everything he typed on his phone." He swallows hard. "So, it turns out there wasn't anything that said you two were gonna get back together. I didn't look at your stuff—but everything in his data told the same story: it was over between you two."

"So you were spying on me? Why did you leak *Wallace's* stuff?"

Jethro takes a long breath. "Anna, I know that what I'm telling you is pretty messed up. . . . I remembered the way they were talking at Wiseguy's, so I went into Wallace's stuff too. If I leaked Palmer's information, people would figure out it was me, once they knew about . . . what happened with *us*. So I dumped Wallace's stuff instead."

"Wow . . . Jethro." I feel like I might throw up.

"It was stupid, Anna. So stupid. But when I saw all the stuff about Palmer using steroids, I just did it without thinking about what could happen. I wanted to hurt him because you loved him. And I needed you to know he isn't who he says he is. Not that I even know what that is anymore. Whatever it was you saw in Palmer—how big-time he is, his looks, whatever it was—I needed you to see that some part of him was bullshit. And I thought when you did, it would be over for good."

The craziest part about all this is, I still haven't told Jethro what I planned to say this morning, when we finally sat down face to face: That I'm through with Palmer. That Jethro and I should give it a go. That I'm in love with him. I was going to tell him that we *can* take the Greyhound bus back and forth from Providence to Boston next year. Now I don't know what to think.

"It just got out of my control," Jethro says. "My leak must've gotten other people digging. Someone figured out how to get in like I did and saw the cache of files, and there was nothing I could do to stop it. I opened Pandora's box, and they copycatted me. I'm not asking for you to forgive me, Anna—I know no one ever will. But I would never have intentionally hurt any of our friends like that. I hope you know that."

"I don't know *anything,*" I sputter.

Jethro stands, walks down the stairs to the bottom. Lights another cigarette. The sun's completely set now, and the only light is coming from a flickering street lamp. It's not just that I've been stunned into silence; I've been stunned into motionlessness too. And I am only beginning to process my own role in all of this.

My phone vibrates. A text.

Searching for any escape route, I check. Only a few

people text me, and they're all my lifelines. What will I tell them? Rad or Nikki or Andrew? With all their lives and friendships in shambles because of what Jethro set in motion, what *could* I tell them?

Anna, it's Vanessa. Tell me if you can talk. We need to talk.

I stare at the screen. Vanessa—asking if I can talk? Is there anyone on earth less likely to be texting me? Anyone I'd rather talk to less right now?

But Vanessa—true to her fashion—waits for no one.

My phone vibrates again. This time, a call. Same number she texted me from.

I answer. "Vanessa, whatever you want from me, I'm not in the mood—"

Only, now I hear sounds on the other end of the line. They cut me short. The sound of *sobs.* From a girl no one even knew had a heart anymore.

Jethro squints at me from the bottom of the stairs, as confused as I am.

Vanessa can barely get words out. "Anna . . . don't hang up. . . . *Palmer is dead.*"

18

WE MET IN AN UNLIKELY PLACE, AT LEAST, UNLIKELY FOR PALMER: the stairwell in front of the art lab. It was the day before the official first day of the school year. I was there at the request of Mr. Touhey to help him and other art faculty members finish a giant *Welcome to Prep* mural to greet new students. There were a few teachers and staff on campus, but it was otherwise empty. Blissfully empty.

Which is why it was so improbable that a blond-haired, blue-eyed boy would crash into me as I stepped out of the art lab with an open, freshly stirred half-gallon can of red acrylic paint in hand. There was no time to react when, out of the corner of my eye, I saw him flying down the steps and into my left elbow, sending a stream of thick, red paint splashing across the second-floor landing.

We looked at each other, stunned. I recognized Palmer immediately, of course. Even though I didn't pay much attention to our basketball team then, he was obviously one of the most talked-about students at Prep. *Everyone* knew Palmer Meade.

"*Oh shit*" was all he said.

I was surprised my nerves weren't flaring more. He was the popular, beautiful boy at school, and we'd just had a really awkward introduction. But a summer of Silver Pines had increased my confidence and stability, I guess. Also, the fact that he didn't say he was sorry immediately really pissed me off.

"Uh, I guess I'll say I was trying out a new Jackson Pollock–esque technique and I . . . missed?" I said, annoyed.

Palmer still didn't say anything, not *sorry* or anything else. He just stood there with a blank look like he could do no wrong.

Typical Insta guy.

I hurried through the art lab and ran into the supply closet, from which I grabbed a handful of rags, a rusty can of Klean Strip, and a small trash can. When I got back, I was surprised to find Palmer still leaning against the wall. And now I saw what I hadn't before. He was breathing very heavily.

"Sorry," Palmer said quietly. "I'm super sorry."

"Uh. It's okay."

I handed a few rags to him, and we got down on our hands and knees, side by side, and started to sop up the mess. "I'm Anna. Anna Soler," I said after a few moments.

"I know," he said between breaths. "Palmer. So . . . sorry."

That's when I realized that something was wrong—

that his heavy breathing wasn't just some pregame technique for taking in more oxygen. Now I could see that his hands were shaking a little, and his face was too red. Even if I didn't know the feeling so intimately myself, I could have seen he was having some kind of panic attack.

He leaned down with his head close to the linoleum floor, trying to steady himself, but it wasn't working.

"Palmer, focus on the sound of my voice, okay?" I said. "Take a deep breath. You're okay. Nice big breath. Now think of the most beautiful, most relaxing place you've ever been in your life."

It took a second, but Palmer leaned up and finally sucked a big gulp of air into his lungs. I could see the sweat beading at his temples.

"Good," I said. "Now let it out slowly. That's it. OK, once more."

By the time the scarlet in Palmer's cheeks and neck faded, we were both sitting on the floor, smack in the middle of the stairwell landing, me cross-legged, him with his long legs splayed out in front of him.

"Better?" I asked.

"Yeah," he sighed, finally lifting his head to meet my eyes.

And it was when we made eye contact that I felt my pulse quicken. "It's no big deal—paint is always getting spilled around here," I managed.

He laughed a little. "We have a preseason game in half an hour. I was trying to find a private bathroom, someplace . . . uh . . ."

"Don't worry about it," I said, not wanting to press him on whatever he was unsure about saying.

"Before games," he said, "I get . . . nervous. I'm a total pregame puker."

"I can't even imagine," I say. "I mean, I can."

"How'd you know about the breathing thing?" he asked.

"Let's just say this isn't my first panic rodeo."

"Gotcha." His deep-blue eyes searched my face, but he didn't press.

"Oh no," he said, looking at the floor. "It looks like a freaking murder scene."

I handed him one of my rags.

He smiled again, and our fingers grazed. The first time our hands had touched.

There was a game I used to play at Six Flags: the guy running the booth gives you a metal loop, and you try to guide it along the curve of a wire without touching the wire. Only I was young, and I couldn't do it well, so when the loop and wire connected by accident, an electric shock—small but sharp—went through my entire body.

According to my laptop, five days have passed.

I haven't left my room since Wednesday night except to see Dr. Bechdel and occasionally sit with my parents at the dinner table. Dad tries to talk about RISD and how bright the future is. Mom's been trying to feed me, but I've eaten a sum total of less than two chicken legs. The shades on my windows are pulled down as far as they'll go, and I'm sleeping in two- to three-hour bursts when the mood strikes, which isn't very often. I definitely haven't been showering. Haven't seen the point.

When Vanessa told me Palmer accelerated his car into a telephone pole on Braddock Road, I blacked out or went into some kind of fugue state or something. Jethro cried when he heard, I think. Like, actually wept. I don't remember where Jethro went then, but Haven (I hear) got me back home to my parents somehow. Apparently I was out of control, crying so hard, wailing. I remember almost none of this, but bits and pieces have been coming back or told to me. I guess once I got home, my mom basically pinned me down and gave me a Xanax from my emergency supply. The "just in case" supply.

Every time I close my eyes, I see Palmer. I think of what I could have done. I should have asked him about his family more. I should have said something that time I heard his dad laying into him, or encouraged him to take it easy after the injury, told him a thousand times more that I cared about him for who he was, not what he did. I should have dragged him to therapy kicking and screaming. And, no matter how many times Dr. Bechdel and other soothing voices tell me this was all a terrible tragedy—that it was *no one's fault*—I feel I share the responsibility.

Even though I haven't set foot on Prep's campus in nearly a week, I'm not out of the loop. My laptop and phone are always in bed with me. My eyes are sore from staring so long. I'm reading through all my feeds, even watching live stuff at school via Facebook Live and Periscope. Timmy Tepper's podcast drones in my room like white noise. Like I said, I don't actually care. I just kind

223

of scroll and listen blindly, like I'm looking for something specific or interesting, only I don't know what that is, exactly.

Mostly it keeps me from thinking too much.

From what I hear, the scene at Prep hasn't gotten any better. You might think it's a good thing that the old cliques have broken down. That the Instagrams and the Future Leaders of America and the Thesbos have been replaced by *We don't have anything in common but at least you didn't stab me in the back* and *Misery loves company and I've lost all my friends* groups. But it's not. It's total chaos.

There have been dozens of new leaks, and the existing ones have grown and twisted and spread like a disease. Every day another signed Auto-Tune remix pops up on Vimeo or YouTube and sweeps the school, reminding everyone of your eating disorder or your best friend you don't trust or how you once asked eHow about gender reassignment surgery. A couple of freshmen have tried to one-up Timmy Tepper and are vlogging about the best ones every night. And people don't even care about staying anonymous anymore. Instead of posting on Yik Yak or Reddit, kids are *taking* credit for their work.

It's like now that our dark sides have been exposed, the dark side seems to be all anyone at Prep wants.

At least . . . that's what it seems like from inside my bedroom.

My friends have texted, DM'd, called, and even stopped by. My mom's not even bothering to ask me if I want to see or talk to anyone anymore. She just tells Nikki or Rad or Andrew or Haven that I need more time.

Mr. Touhey wrote me an actual letter, on the back of a postcard, on the front of which was an old black-and-white photo, by someone named Jacques Henri Lartigue, of a fancy-looking Frenchwoman in furs and a big hat walking two tiny dogs.

> *Hey there, kiddo. I know the last couple of weeks have been rough. But I hope you'll still be able to submit your piece for the show. Ralph Waldo Emerson said, "Always do what you are afraid to do." Not bad advice. Advanced Art is counting on you!*

I tore the postcard in half and tossed it in my wastebasket. I retrieved it a few hours later and taped it back together and put it on my nightstand and stared at it for what must have been hours while tears soaked my pillowcase. (There's been a lot of pillow flipping these days. Cry into one side, flip, cry into other side, flip.)

The one person I *have* talked to a little is Haven. A couple of days ago, I asked my personal tech Svengali to retrieve and send me back all my texts and chats with Palmer. All the cruel messages I had tried to delete to save myself. I wound up saving nobody.

Haven filled me in on what's happening with Jethro, as much as I could bear to listen to. Jethro confessed to the school and police over email that he was responsible for the initial Wallace leak, but he was still staying away. The police are investigating the leaks, trying to determine whether blame is to be shared. This was a group effort, after all. The school scheduling app recording everything, Jethro throwing open the doors, and everyone else feeding on the information, spreading the misery. Nichols and the administration are holding a hearing this week to determine Jethro's fate.

I cut Haven off before he could say anything else.

Thinking about what'll happen to Jethro is the only thing worse than replaying what already happened between us over and over again in my mind. He made his choices, and I don't know if we can ever speak again, but I don't want him to suffer more.

Worse yet, I miss him so badly.

Through the door I hear Mom's voice. "Anna, I'm heading over to the church to pay my respects to Palmer's family. I thought you might have changed your mind. There's still time." She pauses. "Sweetheart, I think you'll regret it if you don't."

I *should* go to Palmer's memorial service. I'll feel bad if I don't go. But I can't go and squeeze into a crowded pew and face all those swarms of people around me who barely knew him saying they're sorry to me. Or talking to me at all. *Memorial service.* Just thinking about it makes my head swim, makes it hard to breathe or see.

"I'll see you later," I tell Mom.

An hour later I'm *watching* Palmer's memorial service.

The Prep administration made the decision to suspend classes for the day, so it appears as if every single student and teacher at Prep is gathered inside the Capitol Hill

United Methodist Church. My guess is that a quarter of the kids are filming. Their Periscope and Facebook Live feeds allow me to cut back and forth between various angles, to see everything that's happening without having to be there.

It takes a couple of minutes, but eventually I see Nikki, sitting with Andrew (who did show up at Mattie Eizenberg's house to beat him up but found out that Mattie's parents had already shipped him off to finish the year at some ruthless military school).

Finally I see Rad. She's sitting in the back with Wallace, believe it or not. Rad's got a hand on his shoulder. I don't know how they have become friends in the past five days. Strange bedfellows, maybe. Or, in Rad's case, I guess, anywhere *but* the bed.

The minister, pale and nervous-looking, stands at the pulpit now, holding up his hands to signal that he's ready to begin. The video quality isn't great, so I can't see anyone clearly. The sound is just as bad. But it's probably best that I can't quite make out what the minister's saying beyond *Death, better place, St. Paul's sermon, First Corinthians.*

I click on Timmy Tepper's live stream.

> *. . . from inside the studio of Pinpoint Productions at 1112 Vermont Avenue in bee-yo-tif-ful Washington, D.C., because Prep Academy is apparently unfamiliar with Amendment Numero Uno. Today I will not be joined by my lovely cohost, Vanessa Eubanks. I don't mind telling you that*

Vanessa and I recently had a difference of opinion. She thought that broadcasting the memorial service was in bad taste. I said to her, "Hey, Vanessa, I have news for you. If I didn't have bad taste, I'd have no taste at all." Several sources at the scene report that—wait a second, folks, hang on, hold your horses, here comes Vanessa right now. She's opening the booth. She's stepping inside the broadcast booth. Vanessa, I thought you'd change your mind, so I left your—

The sound that follows is unmistakable.

A bitch slap.

Followed by the sound of a pair of headphones hitting the floor, skittering across it. Followed by the sound of a cry, high-pitched but unmistakably male. And then Vanessa must yank out a cord, because all of a sudden, there's nothing but dead air.

At least one fair thing has happened in the past few days.

My attention drifts back to the live video feeds. I can tell that the minister's address is over. Palmer's mother has replaced him at the pulpit. As she's speaking, people are starting to cry.

I find Palmer's dad in the front pew and catch my breath. Mr. Meade is bent over his knees, face in hands, shoulders heaving. He's sobbing. The night of the crash, they tried to tell everyone it was an accident. But too many witnesses came forward: he didn't swerve; he looked eerily calm. Finally word got out that there was a note. Only his parents will probably ever know what it said.

I click back to my texts.

Palmer glows at me in thin letters, black-and-white. Here are the random things he wrote to me in those first days, the bad jokes he made, and the sweet emojis he used. There are our thousands of exchanges over the first month, two people with really only one thing in common trying to find anything else we had in common. I keep scrolling. Here are some not-so-nasty things I told Palmer about my friends. Some pride and love I shared with him before I soured with fear and insecurity. Then comes the bad stuff, of course. The cruel, mean stuff that could ruin our friendships forever. That would stop my friends from ever coming to check on me again.

I think about that night Palmer came to my window, how I told him he made a bad choice because he was desperate. That, whatever he'd done, whatever trust he'd broken, the steroids were a thing he did. Not who he was. They weren't the whole picture not even close.

I flip back to the memorial. The service is dismissed by the minister, and now, on a bunch of different video feeds, I see my friends' faces as they stand and wait to file out, see the toll the past couple of weeks has taken on them. Nikki's ignoring Rad. Rad's staring at her ex–best friend and wishing she had something—anything—to say.

Finally my eyes land one last time on Mr. Meade, still hiding his face.

I know what I want to do.

I move toward the light—well, toward the screen on my phone. I pull up Haven's last text and reply:

Can you come over? Need help w something. Thx

He replies seconds later:

On my way

19

"ARE YOU OKAY?" NIKKI WHISPERS IN MY EAR. "I MEAN, OF course I know you're not okay. But are you hanging in?"

"It's good to see you, Nik," I say, avoiding the question.

She's at my front door, tears welling in her eyes. We hug for another few seconds, and I pull her inside. Mom waves from the kitchen, says something to Nikki about how it's good that she's here, and returns to the steamed crabs she's making that have the entire house smelling like the Chesapeake Bay. Mom's been pretty great about not letting her curiosity about everything that's happening overpower my need for privacy.

"This is the cleanest I've ever seen this place, A," Nikki says as I shut my bedroom door behind us.

"You should've been here three days ago."

"I wanted to be."

"I know. I'm sorry. I wasn't ready to talk to anyone."

I reach behind Nikki and grab a manila folder off my desk. It's time. "Do you remember the summer you went to theater camp? That place in Maine?"

She looks surprised. "How the hell do you remember that?"

I offer her the folder. "Because you're not the only one who keeps a box."

A smile creeps across her face as she opens it. It's the first time I've seen that beautiful right-sided dimple in weeks. "You kept all my letters?"

"Of course."

"No wonder we're friends. You're a hoarder, just like me."

I nod. "But, Nik, I need you to read those carefully."

"The summer of my massive, pubescent crush on Bryan Weinstein?" she says, flipping through. "I don't understand."

Nikki pulls her blond hair into a loose knot and drops down onto my bed. Her face falls a little more as she flips pages. Finally she looks up at me, her eyes filled with frustration. "So . . . what?" she says. "You're saying it's okay, what Rad did to me? That I'm just as bad as she is? We were in seventh grade! It's completely different."

"I'm not trying to say you're bad, Nik. I'm trying to say you were *mad*."

Nikki throws the folder back at me, and her letters fan out onto the floor. "We're really talking about this? Now? After everything? Jesus, Anna."

"Do you really remember what happened that summer?"

"I told Rad over the phone about messing around with

Bryan, and she called me an overprivileged white girl who doesn't care about her friends."

"You kissed the only boy she ever liked in middle school," I say. "And then you spent the rest of the summer blaming her for not kissing him first. You wrote some pretty terrible things to me about her."

She glances down at the papers scattered across my bed.

She stares at me. "What do you want, Anna?"

"I want you to come with me."

We go back down through Steamed-Crabville, and I lead her to the basement stairs. The lights are already on, and I walk down first. Nikki reluctantly follows. We spent so many hours of our elementary and middle school years here, and when we get to the bottom, Nikki sees the third member of our girl clan. Rad stands in front of the desktop computer Haven has assembled for me down here.

Nikki spins on her heels. "I'm leaving."

"Nik . . ."

Nikki turns back, venom in her voice. "Why are you doing this?"

I ignore her and look at Rad. "Are you finished reading?"

Rad slinks toward us. "Yeah. Your turn, Nikki."

"To do what?" she asks me, not Rad.

"To show you two who I really am."

Nikki shakes her head. "What are you talking about?"

I move slowly toward the computer monitors. Up on

one of the screens are more than a hundred lines of text. Insults and slights and just plain meanness directed at my best friends, all courtesy of yours truly. "You both say I'm the only real friend either one of you has left," I say. "But if we're real friends, then I need you to see something."

Turning my palm up, I direct it toward one of the monitors. "This is every bad thing I said about either one of you that was recorded on my phone. During the leaks I tried to delete it, but Haven eventually recovered every word. So you could both see it. See that we're all a part of this cruelty. Not just Vanessa, not just Wallace, not just Timmy Tepper. It's you, Rad, and you, Nikki, and certainly me too."

Nikki slowly steps back down the stairs. She holds Rad's gaze for the first time since we came down here, then trains her eyes on the glow of the monitors. After almost a minute of silence, she turns back and looks at Rad. "Are you okay?" she asks.

Rad clears her throat. "I don't know. Are you?"

Now Nikki's gaze meets mine. "I don't know."

I suck in a huge breath—as much air as I can. "Palmer's not dead 'cause he couldn't handle losing a scholarship. And he's not even dead because his parents killed him in their pressure cooker. He's dead 'cause he didn't have any friends he could talk to about what was really wrong with him.

"Well, I'm not going to keep lying to you two and find myself in the same place. I can't tell you what to do, obviously. But I *can* tell you we've all been terrible to each other at *one* point or another in ten years of friendship. Probably me most of all, like just in the past three months."

Rad and Nikki are both staring at the floor.

"I'm sorry," I continue, "but does that mean we should all stop being friends now? Abandon each other at the worst moment in our lives?"

Silence.

Finally Rad glances back at the computer monitors, sighs, then looks at me again. "You're a royal bitch. Like, the bitchiest bitch ever. I should slap you."

I close my eyes.

"I had to say it," Rad continues. "You deserve it. But I'm done. Moving on." She looks over at Nikki. "What about you?"

Nikki pauses for a moment, then slowly nods.

I take another deep breath. "So, um . . . listen, there's one other thing."

20

OKAY, THIS IS INSANE, BUT I'M STANDING BACKSTAGE IN THE Graham Auditorium, and I'm not hyperventilating. Am I nervous? Yes. But it's not enough to stop me. Maybe it's the multiple prep sessions with Dr. Bechdel or the Xanax in my pocket as backup. Or maybe it's that I finally admitted to my best friends—the last, crucial piece of my confession—that I had sex with Jethro.

Talking to Nikki and Rad was a relief. Finally I vented about my fear that I had set in motion a series of events that led to my ex-boyfriend being put in a box and buried. Rad and Nikki, sensible as ever, reminded me that there were a lot of factors. Yeah, they said, maybe I shouldn't have had casual sex with Jethro when he was so obviously in love with me. But I had the right to be honest with him if I wasn't sure about a relationship, and it definitely didn't give him permission to go hacking into Wallace Reid's account and open this whole can of worms. It's all still hard to swallow.

But I feel like I'm finally gaining some perspective.

I peek from backstage and see Mr. Touhey at the podium, introducing me. He's wearing a psychedelic paisley-patterned shirt and an actual blazer and tie. The audience is surprisingly full, given the fact that a quarter of the school seems to be out "sick" every day now. As a way to repair kids' attendance records after all the missed days due to the recent mayhem, Prep is offering a half-day credit to students attending tonight's presentation. I'm searching for familiar faces (other than Mom and Dad, right in the front row) when I notice Mr. Touhey is staring right at me, waving me toward him.

There's hardly any applause as I walk out. Asses have been parked in seats for the better part of an hour now. Besides, Prep kids are too hostile to put their hands together enthusiastically for anything short of Nichols canceling school for the rest of the year. There isn't a person in the audience who hasn't been touched by the leaks.

Some guy in the back yells, *"Silver Pines, Silver Pines!"* to the tune of "Silver Bells." (Rad's data leak let everyone know about my little "vacation" there.)

"Quiet," Nichols says.

"Shut up, *assholes,*" Vanessa yells back from the third row. She stands, glares them into submission, then looks back at me and gives me a motion: *Proceed.*

I give her an appreciative look.

Mr. Touhey always says half of art is the artist presenting her work. And now that I'm bound for art school, I guess I'll have to get used to it. So. Bombs away.

"For most of this year," I begin, "I was working on a portrait of myself that was like a selfie but actually more of a commentary on selfies. When I was working on my self-portrait, I was thinking about how I view myself but also about how everyone else views me. The point I was making is that I have a self-image problem. I mean, who doesn't, right?"

Two sophomore girls in the second row are now arguing audibly about something other than what I'm saying. Someone says, "You mind, ladies?"

My dad's voice. Bless him.

I lean back into the mic, trying not to lose control of the crowd. At an orchestra performance three nights ago, there was an actual brawl among ten students in the audience, and the fire alarm was pulled after one of the trumpet players smashed another guy over the head with his brass. Tonight could easily turn into another one of those.

"Ahem, anyway," I push on, "the last thing you guys need is for me to show you my amateur self-portrait. After all, I'm standing in front of masters. All of you."

"What the hell're you talking about!" someone calls out.

I nod to the stage manager, Karen, and after a couple of awkward seconds of nothing happening, the curtain opens. It's dark onstage, and all people can see behind me now is the silhouette of a ten-foot-tall fort we've built with risers and temporary room dividers, hiding what's inside. To find out, they'll have to walk inside.

That same guy yells out, "It's so beautiful I could cry!"

More laughs.

What he and the other laughers don't know is that inside our little fort, Nikki and her stage crew have helped me set up every giant monitor the theater department has at its disposal and turned the stage into an immersive video experience.

"So. Who wants to go in first?" I ask the crowd.

A few dozen people stand up.

"We are all master self-portraitists online," the first group of ten seniors hears as they begin their journey into the darkened tunnel of connected rooms on the stage. As they walk through the entrance, they're hearing Radhika's voice, prerecorded.

Photographs start fading in and out every few seconds on the video monitors surrounding the group. Instagram, Facebook, Twitter, and Google images—curated pictures, posted on social media by Prep kids, that Haven could scrape off the Web. Happy, shiny, blissful, pre-data-leak photos. Of parties, of sports events, of vacations the rest of the world can be jealous of. Kids whisper and point and giggle when they see themselves or their friends flash up on the walls.

"We share these photos that have been taken from flattering angles with Valencia or Mayfair filters," Rad continues as the kids wade their way into the second room of the video maze. "That show us having maximum fun with the coolest people we can get to hang out with us."

Photos of Palmer spread across the screens now. Some are from his social media and press photos, some I took at the basketball game, some are candids of him and his friends, him and me, him and everyone else.

The freshman drama kids Nikki has helping us usher the group forward, into the next room, the final in the installation.

"And it's not just our *photos*," Nikki's voice says. "Every word we post or tweet or snap is crafted and edited and obsessed over too. We all know what people say about social media. They say our public, online selves don't show our true selves or what we really think about our friends."

Comments kids have made on social media start popping up on the screens, fading in and out: *You hot playa* and *Where u get that outfit* and *wish I were in Cairo wif u, jealous* and *bae and 1/2* and *puuuuuuurrrrty* and *literally flawless* and *mah two faves* and *ur perfect* and *Ugh I want to be in pic* and *Omg crop me in* and *Wouldn't want to have grown up w anyone else.*

Nikki's voice rings through the room again. "They're almost all kind, sweet, flattering little notes written to people, humble brags, or stuff dashed off to make us look funny, self-deprecating, cool. But none of these were really dashed off at all, the cynics say. They were all *written*. Put out there for your friend and the public to see."

"So what do we *really* think about each other?" my voice sneaks in as the social media posts finish. "About ourselves? About each other? Well, people say the leaks have finally showed everyone else the truth about what we think and who we really are. We are bad friends, bad boyfriends and girlfriends, and not one of us is being real about who we are, even to the people we're supposed to care about. So let's take a look."

Phrases and emojis start popping up fast on the screens, simultaneously read aloud by me, Nikki, Rad, Haven, Andrew, even Vanessa: *such a bitch* and *f her* and *what a slut* and *I h8 him* and *with frenemies like her* and *need blow job will pay* and *I M depressed* and *he was scamming with that cunt* and *u wanna hookup* and *she's on the bulimia train* and *it's 420 yo, let's check in* and *Oxy rules need more* and *I M done w/her* and *I beat his faggot ass* and even the occasional N-word. It gets worse and worse. It gets stomach-churning.

"These are all from texts and chats and DMs and anonymous comments and anything else exposed in the last two weeks," I say as Rad's recorded voice reads another, one I know well: *worst writer on the paper, how is she editor?*

The seniors were laughing when it started. Now, a minute later, by the time they've seen *thousands* of these messages flash across the screen—some of which were written about them—it's less funny. A few dozen rape threats and death threats and some hate speech later, there isn't a smile or snicker left in the group.

Finally, the nastiness stops. The screens go black again.

"By our count," I say then, "including a few that could be interpreted either way, we wrote a total of three thousand, four hundred seventy-eight terrible things about each other in the data that was leaked. And because these are shocking, and negative, and pretty terrible, it's easy to focus on them entirely," I say. "It's easy to imagine that those are what we *really* think. That's how the human brain works—it holds on to the negative. But here's the thing. That number is *nothing* compared with the positive things we wrote."

Phrases and emojis return to the screens, and our voices fill the space. Only now what's being read aloud are things like *ur the best* and *don't worry you're a* ☆ and *come find me after 4th* and *he don't deserve u* and *ur not alone* and *she's wicked* 😎 and *can I help?* and *we should let her come or she'll be* 😢 and *he* 🏀*s like a playa* and *can you tutor me in geom?* and *it's gonna be off the* 🔄*, can't do it without u* and *whatup new b-fry* and *I'm here 4 u forevs.*

As my friends' voices continue, mine comes in over the top again. "We bitch about each other, share secrets and gossip, and we're bad friends to each other sometimes. Sometimes. But if the data tells a story, it's not that we're monsters. It's that most of the time, we look out for each other and check in on each other and keep each other's spirits up. It's that the nasty things we dash off when we're frustrated or sad or pissed at our friends aren't the *real* us any more than our Instagram comments are the real us. If the leaks tell our true story, it's that we're more back havers than backstabbers. Six thousand, nine hundred ninety positive things we said to each other can't be wrong. That's twice as many good ones as there are bad ones."

The kids standing inside the installation are frozen still, mesmerized by the absurd amount of positivity flashing before their eyes.

"You need more proof?" my prerecorded voice continues. "If you count all the ways we signify it, all the ways we emoji and write and shorthand it, can you guess which word was used most often when you combine all the data that was leaked over the last two weeks? You won't even believe it. You'll probably throw up in your mouth when you hear it. But it's also the ridiculous, sickly sweet truth about us saps. *This* word is what we think and write about most."

LOVE appears on the screen.

Then a 🖤.

And six 😍 🤍 💞.

Then fifty more *LOVE*s.

A hundred more 👩‍❤️‍💋‍👨 💘 🖤 💝 😻.

Almost every kid is smiling now. Probably some of them are embarrassed. But they also realize what we realized when we started sifting through all the data: that our embarrassment doesn't make it any less true.

A minute later, the total number of times the word *LOVE* or a heart emoji appeared in the exposed data is covering every inch of the room's walls.

"Fourteen thousand, nine hundred and eighty-seven times, one of you used that word in your secret texts and DMs," I tell them finally. "How cheesy is that? I mean, really, who are you people?"

Epilogue

"If we shadows have offended,
Think but this, and all is mended,
That you have but slumber'd here
While these visions did appear.
And this weak and idle theme,
No more yielding but a dream . . ."

If you can believe it, that's Haven.

It's been two months since the art show, and by some *we're all in this together, High School Musical* miracle, *A Midsummer Night's Dream* is going off without a hitch—without so much as a heckle. (Okay, maybe a chuckle or catcall here and there, but compared with what this place was not long ago, it's way tame.)

Nikki's half the reason why; she threw herself into the

production, taking on much more than the sets, practically hip checking the drama teacher and stage manager out of her way and making this happen by sheer force of will. Her friends, old and new, are the other half: we were all happy to help her banish the memory of Mattie Eizenberg and his Puck out of existence in whatever way we could. I even did my part by putting all my post-art-show energy into painting the sets.

Haven's impishness has found a perfect home in Puck. He's filling in for the scum who shall not be named, to "branch out" and keep distance from his dad, who he's still not talking to. And, I think, like me, to keep his mind off his still-MIA best friend.

"Where's Reek?" Nikki whispers behind me.

"You said no bows for her."

"Oh right," she says. "Gotta take advantage of the final night." Nikki nods curtly. It makes me so happy to see that her confidence is back.

Reek, the artist formerly known as Radhika, has subjected herself to being Nikki's right-hand slave/personal assistant the past couple of months in order to make up for what she did. Her contract ends tonight, with this final curtain. It's been grueling for Rad, but she's taken it like a champ. Plus, right after the art show, the *Xandria* got to run a special commentary issue about the leaks, and people are saying Rad's gonna get some kind of student Pulitzer for it or something. She wrote brilliantly about the school's terrible technology practices while commenting on the culture of our generation and how we all have to share not only the blame for what happened but the responsibility for picking up the pieces. Shame on me for *ever* saying Rad couldn't write.

The leaks cast a spell over us, had Prep bewitched in some weird, hostile trance. The art show didn't exactly snap things back to normal, but I think it was the first blink out of our collective hypnosis. Some friends, like me and Nikki and Rad, quietly made amends, while others didn't. For the most part, social groups, with little fuss or fanfare, re-formed, reclaimed their tables in the dining hall. People aren't any nicer or meaner than they were before the leaks. If anything, I think everyone is a little more private, a little less trigger happy with the Post and Comment buttons. I wonder how long it will last.

I still haven't heard from Jethro. No one has since we found out Palmer was dead. I've sent him DMs and texts, even tried to call him once, but a random woman answered; he's given up his number entirely. Jethro's mom, afraid of repercussions or getting SWATed like Haven and his dad did, I guess, is in New York with his grandmother. I called once but hung up in a panic when she answered.

Maybe one day I'll be ready to try her again.

Dr. Bechdel tells me that sometimes closure is one sided. It's in the letting go rather than the resolution. So that's what I'm working on. It doesn't matter how I may or may not feel about Jethro—about *us;* I may never see him again. The only thing I can control is how I think about that.

"So, good night unto you all," Haven bellows into the audience.

"Give me your hands, if we be friends,
And Robin shall restore amends."

The lights dim, the curtain closes, and the audience applauds thunderously. Haven, it turns out, is just as good an actor as he is a hacker. People whoop and whistle. Finally, the curtain opens again, and the lights come back up for the cast to take their bows. After they're done, Nikki leads the stage crew out, grabbing my wrist on the way. The roar of the audience—the sound of positivity and support—feels surreal.

In the lobby, cast, crew, and audience mingle. I stand near Andrew, behind the concessions table. He, some of his fellow outed athletes, and their supporters are managing the concessions and programs. All profits from the play are going to a memorial fund benefiting at-risk teens.

From my wallflower position, I watch people chatting, hugging, congratulating one another. Nikki is on the other side of the room, talking and laughing with a stage-crew/debate-team guy. The guy is tall, and gangly, and so shy, I've never actually heard him speak, but Nikki looks happy.

Wallace, a full head taller than most of the crowd, finds a very sweaty Reek/Rad, who's just finished closing down the sets as her final task from Nikki, and gives her flowers. I've never seen the big lug so smitten—or Rad so flustered around a boy. It turns out, when no one else would sit with them in the cafeteria—when Nikki was still avoiding Rad, when members of the basketball team could barely look at one another after their MVP died—they wound up sitting together. However weird it is, it's actually working.

"Hey, creeper."

Rad stands in front of me, Wallace trailing behind her.

"How does it feel to have broken free of the chains of bondage?" I ask.

Rad exchanges a look with Wallace, and they laugh at the word. I don't know if Wallace has managed to give Rad all the experience she never had over the past month or so, but I've been encouraging Rad to keep those things to herself for now, either way.

"Oh God," I say. "Please don't put that image in my head."

Just then Haven walks up behind them—still in his tights.

"That was money," Wallace tells him.

"Dude," Andrew says. "You should change out of those. It's weird."

"Don't knock 'em till you try 'em," Haven says, winking.

"You should wear 'em to the party," Rad says. And then, to me: "See you there?"

"Gotta stop home first," I say, pointing to the paint all over my shirt from last-minute touch-ups, "but I'll be there."

I'm nervous but excited for the cast-and-crew party, to spend time with my friends and the people who worked so hard to pull this off despite all that's happened.

"I'm *home*," I call out to my parents as I dump my bag by the door.

They're drinking wine in the kitchen. Mom rushes in and says how wonderful the show was. Dad tells me he loved my sets, but he doesn't think Shakespeare was much of a comedian. "I prefer the tragedies," he says with a laugh.

Suddenly we're wrapped in a group hug. As much as I can't wait to get out of Northern Virginia and the craziness of this year, I'll miss these two weirdos.

Upstairs, I throw on a fresh pair of jeans and the only clean, cute sweater I can find. I put on lipstick and place a few bobby pins in my hair. I'm ready to blow back out, but just as I'm about to close my bedroom door, something on my desk catches my eye.

Topping off the pile of papers and schoolwork is a postcard.

I walk back in and pick it up. It's a sepia-toned artist's drawing of two llamas standing beneath massive sand dunes that rise above a lake. My heart skips as I turn over the card. Foreign stamps and postmarks that cover the top right corner say:

Huacachina, Peru

On the left side of the card is an unsigned message in familiar handwriting:

*We can sandboard together, all the way down
to the bottom.*

About the Author

JILLIAN BLAKE grew up in New England, where she kept her deepest, darkest secrets password-protected. *Antisocial* is her first novel.